THE TARTAN RAINBOW

with a foreword by
Theresa Breslin

Illustrated by
Samuel Hearn

D1589391

MACMILLAN CHILDREN'S BOOKS

First published 2002 by Macmillan Children's Books
A division of Macmillan Publishers Limited
20 New Wharf Road, London N1 9RR
Basingstoke and Oxford
www.panmacmillan.com

Associated companies throughout the world

ISBN 0 330 39921 7

1 3 5 7 9 8 6 4 2

A CIP catalogue record for this book is available from the British Library.

Typeset by SX Composing DTP, Rayleigh, Essex
Printed and bound in Great Britain by Mackays of Chatham plc, Kent

To Kathleen, who sees rainbows
TB

CONTENTS

FOREWORD

I've been writing stories now for thirteen years (thirteen very lucky years) and during that time I've met hundreds and hundreds of young people, along with parents, carers, librarians and teachers.

When we talk together about reading we all agree that it is very hard to decide on the best book to read. How do you know if a story is an interesting one? Is there any way to tell whether it will be exciting enough to read right to the end? And there are so many different kinds of stories to choose from: adventure, fantasy, mystery, scary. Surely a book can't have *all* of these in it? Then Macmillan Children's Books asked me for help with their great idea – to put together all types of stories in an exciting collection. We asked top writers for brand-new stories with enjoyment a 'must'.

Scotland is a vibrant place to be at the moment for reading and writing. The huge Edinburgh Book Festival takes place every year in August. Scottish Book Trust promotes authors and events. Reading and writing clubs for young people are being set up in libraries and schools all over the country. We have dozens of good writers, some born in Scotland, some born elsewhere but brought up in Scotland, and some who decided to move to Scotland and liked it so much that they have never left. Our writers are on islands, in cities and in the countryside; there are those who still live in Scotland and those who don't.

I'd like to thank them all for their stories, and thanks to you, the reader, for choosing this book. Dip in and try it out. You'll find daft dads and polite pirates, animals with attitude and stories about settling in at school. There are tales of monsters, dog-nappers, island raft races, football, eccentric teachers, brownie magic, holidays, odd aunties, steaming cowpats, baby otters and the mysterious orange man.

These stories will make you laugh, make you think and make you want to read them again. Each one is different, with its own pattern, part of a dazzling range spread out among the sparkling illustrations for you to enjoy.

A bit like a rainbow . . . a tartan rainbow.

Theresa Breslin

I WENT TO LOCH NESS IN SEARCH OF A MONSTER BUT ALL THAT I FOUND THERE WAS YOU

Keith Gray

My cousin Barry is a real pain. He's small and runty with spiky hair. He had to leave his first primary school when he stole the teacher's mobile phone and sent rude text messages to everybody in the phone's memory. He tried to run away with the circus once. And just this year he went to his school's fancy dress party as a hooded executioner and tried to behead two little kids in the assembly hall.

And I know what you're thinking: I'm ten, two years older than Barry, so why should I care what he does? Well, you've not met him. Think yourself lucky. He's horrible.

I'll tell you about last year's holiday and then maybe you'll see what I mean.

Every year Mum, Dad, Katie and I have to spend a weekend in Cornwall or the Lake District or somewhere with Auntie Sarah and Barry. We have done ever since Uncle Jerry died. Dad says it's the only chance he gets to see his sister.

My dad works away from home a lot, and last year he'd been spending loads of time in Scotland. He told us it was the most beautiful scenery he'd ever seen and he wanted us all to see it too. I always worry when Dad says 'beautiful scenery' because it means no shops, no arcades, no roller coaster. It means long walks even if it's raining. But then Dad said we'd be staying in a town called Fort Augustus at the southern end of Loch Ness, and that sounded much more exciting.

'Can I borrow your camera, Dad?' I asked. 'And your binoculars? I want to photograph the monster and be famous!'

We stayed in this little guesthouse with nasty wallpaper on the main road through Fort Augustus. It was called the Caledonian Cottage and was packed with tourists from all over the world. Mum and Dad had one room, Auntie Sarah and Katie another. Which meant I had to share with Barry.

I tried to complain. 'But, Dad . . .'

He didn't listen.

'It's awful sleeping in the same room as Barry,' I said.

'You're just being unfriendly,' he told me.

Me? He didn't understand. Sleeping with Barry is the worst ever, because he *cackles*. It's awful. In the dark, in the middle of the night, when everything else is quiet, he cackles to himself as he dreams up his horrible schemes. And having to listen to it sends creepy pins and needles up your spine.

I started to worry as soon as we got into our room. Barry closed the door and locked us in. 'This is gonna be the best holiday *ever*,' he said, rolling his eyes, rubbing his hands together, and grinning like a burglar with somebody else's TV.

He tipped his suitcase upside down in the middle of the floor, spilling his clothes everywhere, not caring that it had only taken him five seconds to make a mess. He burrowed through them until he found what he was looking for. 'See what I've got.' He had a silver camera about the size of his hand. 'Cool, yeah?' he beamed, pressing a button to make the lens zoom in and out with a whirring sound.

'What d'you want that for?' I asked (as if I didn't already know). I was jealous because Dad's camera didn't whirr.

'I'm going to photograph the monster,' he said, still grinning.

'But that's what *I* want to do.'

He shrugged his shoulders. 'So, you can help me if you want.' He pointed the camera at me. 'Say "cheese".' And he took my picture as I pulled a sulky face. 'Don't crack the lens,' he said.

I was dead mad, because it had been my idea and Barry had just stolen it. I tried to get Katie on my side by asking her to help me, but she said she had better things to do than look for monsters. So I told Dad.

'Barry wants to photograph the monster, and he's got a camera that's better than mine. He must have stolen it.'

'It was his birthday present,' Dad said. 'Why don't you work together? Four eyes are better than two, after all.'

But he only said that because he has to wear glasses.

We went to Castle Urquhart, where most people have been when they've seen the monster. The drive from Fort Augustus to the castle is amazing, all along the side of the loch on this winding road. And the loch itself is massive. I was expecting a big, round lake, but it's really long, like the widest river you've ever seen. The hills on either side are tall, with trees coming right down to the water. Boats out in the middle look tiny.

I enjoyed exploring the castle. It was built hundreds of years ago and kind of sticks out over the loch. Barry scratched his name in the wall with a stone, then pretended it was his prehistoric ancestor who'd done it years and years ago. I took no notice, because all the time the water seemed to keep making me look at it. It pulled my eyes towards it. And I could almost feel the monster watching me. Just at the corner of my vision I kept seeing dark ripples far out from the shore. Was it a hump?

At last Dad let Barry and I go down to the water with our cameras. There wasn't really a beach or anything. The ground slopes down a little and it's all pebbles and rocks, with scrubby bits of grass. I was surprised by how dark the water was. It was a bright sunny day, but the water was almost black.

We both stared out into the middle. My finger was always ready on the button. I did take a couple of pictures, but only to make Barry think I'd seen it. He took loads, trying to fool me. *Whirr, whirr,* every five minutes.

Then he got bored after about half an hour and pushed me in.

I was soaked and freezing, and I scraped my knees on the rocks when I fell because I'd been trying to stop my camera from getting wet. I was so angry that I nearly cried. Barry laughed; I hated him. So we had a fight, right at the water's edge. But Barry's a better fighter than me – he's had more practice – and he pushed me in again.

Dad was really mad. Mum said we were spoiling the holiday for everybody. Auntie Sarah took Barry's camera off him and said he could only have it back when he started to behave. I thought that was funny.

After I'd dried off we spent the afternoon in the nearby town called Drumnadrochit, at a Loch Ness Monster Exhibition. It was OK, but I'd seen all the photos before. What did surprise me was when Mum said she didn't believe in the monster. Both Barry and I were amazed: there are photos!

That night Barry still wasn't allowed his camera back so he sulked all the way through dinner. Auntie Sarah told him off when he said the meat in his steak and ale pie was alive and moving. Then he asked for extra gravy and pretended to get drunk on the ale it was made with. Everybody else in the restaurant stared at us, and Barry got told off again, not that he cared. He went to bed early, but I woke up in the middle of the night to find him rooting through my rucksack.

I leaped out of bed. 'What're you doing?'

'Looking for this.' In a flash he'd grabbed my camera and was climbing out of the window. 'I'm going to photograph the monster.'

'But that's *my* camera!' I complained. 'And it's the middle of the night. Dad'll go crazy!' But he didn't wait to listen, so I had to follow him. 'I want to hold the camera,' I said. 'It's *my* camera.'

It was three o'clock, not too cold, with lots of stars in the sky. We ran all the way along the silent main road down to the loch. Fort Augustus has a tiny little harbour with yachts and fishing boats for tourist trips, and this was where we headed. I didn't realize what Barry planned to do at first, but he wanted to steal somebody's row-boat and get right out into the middle of the water. That's where he thought he had the best chance to see the monster. He reckoned it probably came out more at night too. I know I should have stopped him, because I am the oldest and the most sensible, but he did have my camera and wouldn't give it back to me.

There was no one around. We crept along the narrow wooden pier between the bigger boats, which were bobbing quietly. He quickly untied one of the small row-boats and we were out on the water in only a few minutes.

'You row and I'll take the photos,' he told me.

'But it's my camera,' I said.

'You're better at rowing than me,' he said. Which was true, because I'd done lots of it at scout camp.

It was really weird out on the loch. Everything was dead silent, apart from us breathing and the slapping sound the water made against the little boat as it bobbed up and down. It was so dark away from the street lights we couldn't see each other's faces properly. I wished we'd brought a torch. I reckoned if my mum was there she would have believed in monsters too. It was spooky and dark and quiet. Both Barry and I talked in whispers. We stared all around us, peering at the black water and the shadowy hills. Every time a wave rocked the boat we held our breath and gripped the sides in case it was the monster swimming underneath us.

'Can you see anything?' I asked.

'No,' Barry whispered. Then he suddenly

shouted, 'What's that? What's that?'

I jumped in my seat, making the row-boat rock crazily. 'What? Where?' I was so surprised I nearly dropped an oar.

'Fooled you,' Barry laughed.

I hated him. I grabbed for my camera back, but he fought me off.

And it was an accident, it really was. He must have slipped. I didn't do it on purpose. He fell backwards as we fought. He tried to push me away but tipped backwards and fell into the water.

I couldn't see him. I could hear him splashing and trying to shout as he struggled to swim, so I used an oar for him to get hold

of, but he couldn't reach it. Every time I stood up the row-boat felt like it was going to tip me in too. I did shout his name, over and over again. He couldn't get back in, and the boat was drifting away. There were lifejackets under the seat and I threw them all in. Then I tried to row in a circle to get to him. I tried really hard but I couldn't do it quickly enough, and couldn't see properly. It was pitch-black. I was the most frightened I'd ever been. It felt like a big cold hand was crushing my chest and making me cry. And soon I couldn't even hear him any more.

All I could do was row back to Fort Augustus as fast as I could. I aimed for the street lights. It seemed to take for ever. My hands hurt with blisters and my arms ached so much, they burned. Then I ran all the way back to the guesthouse and got Dad. I was so scared I couldn't stop crying. Everything seemed like a blur. I knew Dad would tell me off, but first he got the police and went out on the loch with them in a boat with a massive searchlight.

Auntie Sarah and Katie cried. Mum was white like milk and really quiet. The police asked me loads of questions. I was crying so much I don't think they understood me because they asked the same ones over and over again. Someone said that if Barry didn't drown he might die because the water was so cold. But that wasn't what worried me.

'What if the monster eats him?' I asked. 'The monster might get him.' I wished so hard I'd stayed in bed.

It was nearly morning now and everybody looked as frightened as I was. The loch was full of boats, and it seemed like the whole town was out searching along the shore. Even some tourists were trying to help.

It was a fat American man called Gus who found Barry. He spotted him trying to sneak back into the guesthouse. And Barry even tried to lie, saying he'd been in bed all the time, because he didn't want to get into trouble. But he was soaking wet and dirty, so he had to admit that he'd used one of the lifejackets I'd thrown in as a float and kicked for shore. He'd climbed up the side through the trees and run along the road, wanting to get back into bed without anybody noticing.

Everybody was so pleased to see him again. Auntie Sarah gave him a massive hug and cried even more. Dad said he was probably the luckiest boy alive, while Gus the American said it was a miracle he'd survived. But I knew it was something else.

He was on the news on TV and in the papers and everything. It was like he was suddenly famous. He told this story about how he'd seen the monster when he'd fallen in. He said it hadn't attacked him, it had helped him by pushing him towards the shore. Nobody believed him, of course. Except for me.

I believe he saw the monster. And I believe it pushed him to the shore too. Because there's only room in Loch Ness for one monster after all, and Nessie was probably scared of the competition.

THE TROUBLE WITH BARNABY

Joan Lingard

The trouble with Barnaby started the moment they arrived at Granny's house in the Highlands. Granny was watching for them at the gate when they turned the bend in the road. And lying along the top of the gate beside her was Barnaby himself.

As if sensing another animal, the cat curled himself up into a ball and hissed. Danny, now awake and up on his four legs on the back seat, began to bark.

'Shush, Danny!' said Joe.

'That's enough, Barnaby!' said Granny.

The cat went on hissing and spitting and the dog went on barking and trying to climb through the car window.

'I was afraid of this,' said Joe's mum.

'We'd better leave Danny in the car,' said Joe's dad.

'We can't leave him in the car all day and all night,' protested Joe.

'I mean for the moment. We'll open the window a couple of inches so that he'll have some air.'

Granny carried a struggling Barnaby into the house while the visitors unpacked and brought in their luggage.

In the sitting room, doing a jigsaw on the floor, was Susie, Joe's cousin.

'Hello, Susie, love,' said Joe's mum, bending down to give her a kiss. 'You're staying with Grammy for a few days, aren't you?'

Joe hadn't known that. If he had he would have asked if he and Danny could stay at Auntie Muriel's, his mum's younger sister.

When they got upstairs, his mum said, 'Be nice now to Susie. Her mum's going to have a new baby. She's had to go down to the hospital in Glasgow early. She's having a wee bit of a problem. Susie's dad has gone with her.'

Since Susie was staying in the house Joe had to sleep in the boxroom, which had no proper window, only a skylight.

'Why should she have *my* room?' he demanded.

'It's not really your room, Joe. It's just the one you usually stay in. But Susie has been here for a few days already so it was only natural she should have the bigger room.'

'I hope the baby's born soon,' he muttered.

He took food and water out to Danny. 'Don't worry your head about Barnaby,' he told him. 'The trouble with him is he's old and crotchety.'

His dad came to join them and suggested

taking Danny for a walk. As soon as the dog heard the word 'walk' he started to bark.

They took him into a nearby empty field and let him have a good run. He was a frisky golden retriever, a puppy still, only six months old. He ran and ran until he collapsed among the daisies and clover, his tongue lolling out.

'Now what will we do with him?' asked Joe.

'I'm afraid you'll have to put him in your room.'

Danny didn't like that one little bit. As soon as Joe left him he began to bark and hurl himself at the door. He barked and barked and, downstairs, Barnaby, who was sitting in his basket with his ears pricked, hissed and snarled and spat.

'I don't know what you had to bring that stupid dog with you for,' said Susie.

'He's not stupid,' said Joe. 'It's that horrible cat's fault.'

Susie stroked Barnaby's ear and he rolled over on to his back so that she could tickle his tummy. He was purring now. 'See, he's really quite a gentle cat. Barnaby and me are friends, aren't we, Barnaby?'

Joe went back upstairs to try to calm Danny down. Some holiday this was going to be! He sat on the floor and stroked

Danny's silky ears and talked to him. He looked round when the door opened.

'Granny and I have been talking,' said his dad. 'And we think we must try to introduce the two animals to each other.'

'I can't see them *ever* being friends,' said Joe, but he took Danny downstairs and out into the yard. As soon as Granny appeared with Barnaby in her arms, both the cat and the dog started to struggle and try to get loose.

'It's all right, Barnaby,' said Granny in a soothing voice. 'Nice Danny.'

'It's all right, Danny,' said Joe. 'Barnaby's a friend.' The word all but stuck in his throat.

'It's never going to work,' remarked Susie from the sidelines.

'Now try taking them a little closer to each other,' said Joe's dad.

Joe and Granny inched towards each other. The animals' eyes were almost out on stalks and the hair on the cat's back stood up like a ridge.

'Go on reassuring them,' encouraged Joe's dad.

Joe and Granny went on stroking the two animals and speaking to them in quiet voices. There was only a small gap between them now. For a moment there was silence and peace. Then Barnaby flew out of Granny's arms and dived at Joe and Danny with claws extended. Joe whirled around to avoid the attack and Danny sprang free and went for the cat. Susie screamed. There was pandemonium while the cat chased the dog and the dog chased the cat and everyone tried to catch them. Joe's dad managed to rescue Danny, who was no match for a furious cat, and Barnaby took refuge up a tree.

'Told you it wouldn't work,' said Susie.

Danny had a small tear on one ear.

'He's a horrible, nasty cat,' said Joe.

'I'm sorry,' said Granny. 'The trouble is that Barnaby thinks this is his territory.'

'Well, it is,' said Susie.

Danny had his ear bathed and was banished once more to the boxroom where he quickly fell asleep, exhausted, no doubt, from the fray. When Joe went downstairs he found Susie in the sitting room on her own.

'Want a game of Snap?' she asked.

'No.'

'I don't know why you didn't go to Auntie Muriel's with your silly dog.'

He left the room and went out into the passage. He was about to open the kitchen door when he heard his mother and grandmother speaking about Susie and himself.

'It's a pity they don't get on better,' said his mum.

Granny sighed. 'I wish they weren't so jealous of each other.'

Him jealous of Susie? How bananas could you get!

He let himself out by the front door and went round to the yard where Barnaby was eating his supper. Joe gave him a small, sly kick, not too big a one, but just enough to let him know that he wasn't going to get away with scratching his dog's ear. The cat stopped eating for a moment to glare at him with his green eyeballs before turning back to his bowl.

His mother appeared at the back door. 'Why don't you have a game of ping-pong with Susie?' she said. There was a table in the garage.

'Don't want to.'

He kicked a ball around the yard until he heard Danny barking, then he went up and put his lead on and brought him downstairs. He stuck his head round the sitting room door.

'I'm going to take Danny for a walk up the lane.'

'Why don't you ask Susie to go with you?' suggested his dad. They were always suggesting something.

'She must be missing her mother,' added his mum.

Joe didn't say anything, he just shrugged and headed off up the lane.

Halfway along there was Barnaby sitting on the branch of a tree beside the cottage where Susie lived with her mother and father. He was here, there and everywhere, that cat. When he saw Joe and Danny he hissed and craned his neck to look down at them, but made no move to jump. Danny, naturally enough, started to bark.

'Stop!' commanded Joe.

'He doesn't pay much attention, does he?' said Susie. Joe hadn't noticed her. She was sitting on the front step of her house.

'He does so! Anyway, he's young and just learning.'

Susie sniffed. She wasn't crying, was she? She couldn't be, not *her*. Joe walked on, dragging a reluctant dog behind him. Danny would much rather have stayed and eyed the cat.

Joe was glad when it was time to go to bed so that he and Danny could settle down in peace for a while.

In the morning, when he awoke, it felt stuffy in the little room so he dressed and took Danny out. He decided not to put the lead on as there was no sign of Barnaby, who was probably still curled up in his warm basket in the sitting room.

It was a lovely morning. The sun was shining on the fields and lighting up the purple heather on the hills. Danny romped through the damp grass, his golden tail swishing from side to side. Joe had to run to keep up with him.

Up ahead, out of a hole, suddenly popped a plump rabbit. For a second it stopped, fixed to the spot, staring at the dog, then off it went at a wild canter with Danny racing after it.

'Danny!' called Joe, but Danny was not listening. He was galloping across the meadow as if Barnaby himself were after him. And then he and the rabbit disappeared into the pine wood at the back of the field.

Joe called Danny's name over and over and over again before going back to the house to tell them what had happened. 'Danny will never be able to find his way out of the wood!' It was a dark, dense, scary wood. Among the new, fresher trees were lots of old ones whose skinny branches looked like witches' fingers.

'I can't find Barnaby, either,' said Granny. 'He likes to go out in the early morning but he always comes back for his breakfast.'

They set out for the wood: Joe, his mum and dad, and Susie.

'You don't have to come.' Joe scowled at her.

'It's my wood,' she said.

'You don't own it.'

'It's at the back of our house.'

'That doesn't mean it's yours.'

'Joe, that's enough,' said his dad. 'Let's concentrate on finding Danny.'

Saying proved to be easier than doing. The wood was riddled with dozens of little paths, deer tracks, mostly, that wound their way between the trees. At one point they disturbed a deer, a young buck, who paused momentarily with his head cocked, to gaze at them before vaulting lightly over a fallen branch and disappearing. He had made scarcely a whisper of sound.

'We must watch that *we* don't get lost,' said Joe's dad. 'Let's stand still for a moment and listen.'

Small birds were twittering in the high branches. Tits, probably. They heard the call of a cuckoo somewhere far off. Now came a rustle. It could have been a vole, or some other small animal. Apart from that it was very quiet in the shadowy dark-green and grey wood.

Then Joe's mum said, 'Listen! I think I can hear something.'

They listened.

'I think it's a cat,' cried Susie. 'I think it's Barnaby!'

They stayed still and listened again, to try to find out from which direction the sound was coming.

'It seems to be this way,' said Joe's dad, going ahead down one of the paths.

The further they went the louder grew the sound. They walked faster. Ahead was a patch of light. They reached a small clearing among the trees where a pile of logs had been stacked by foresters. And there was Barnaby sitting on guard beside a whimpering Danny! They quickly saw that the dog's left leg was trapped under a heavy log, which must have rolled off the pile. Barnaby was in the middle of licking the puppy's face. At once the cat sat back as if he didn't want them to see what he had been doing. He ignored them and began to lick his paw and wash his own face.

'Danny!' cried Joe, rushing up to him.

'Careful now,' cautioned his dad. 'We must release his leg gently.'

Danny whimpered even more loudly while his leg was being freed. Joe's dad carried him out of the wood, cradled in his arms. Joe walked beside them, stroking Danny's head and telling him he was going to be all right. Barnaby followed behind.

They took Danny to the vet in the village, who X-rayed the leg and, finding it was fractured, bound it up in a splint.

'It'll mend quickly,' he said cheerfully. 'He's a young dog.'

When they returned home Susie met them at the gate. 'Is he OK?' She held out a chocolate biscuit for Danny, who brightened and wolfed it down quickly.

Joe noticed that Susie had a big smile on her face.

'Guess what?' she said. 'My mum's had a wee girl.'

Joe groaned inwardly. Not another *girl* cousin.

'That's fantastic,' said his dad. 'Isn't it, Joe?'

Joe grunted something, and they went into the house.

Granny had found for Danny a spare cat basket, which she had lined with a soft, sunshine-yellow, lambswool blanket. Joe's dad laid him gently in it. Barnaby was sitting in his basket, on the other side of the hearth. The animals looked at each other. Neither made a sound. Granny heaved a sigh of relief, plainly heard by everyone.

'Fancy a game of Snap?' asked Susie.

'Go on, Joe, give her a game,' urged his mum.

'Oh, OK.'

They squatted, cross-legged, on the floor opposite each other.

'Do you want to deal?' asked Susie.

'No, you can.'

She dealt and they picked up their cards. But before they started they glanced over at Danny and Barnaby. Both were sleeping peacefully in their own baskets. Joe and Susie grinned at each other and began to play.

THE ORANGE MAN

Jackie Kay

One day in the middle of winter, my grandmother told me about the orange man. Outside, snow was thick on the ground, lying still in silence. The trees in Alexander Parade had crispy branches. They looked as if you could just snap them off. It was brrrrrr cold. Not just cold, but freezing. I was inside in my grandmother's warm tenement flat, up on the second floor. From her window I could see the Glasgow Royal Infirmary, ambulances coming and going.

A real coal fire was sparking and roaring in one of her two rooms, but her story was making me cold. I was frightened. The thing that frightened me most was that my grandmother's story was true. All her stories were true. That is what she says: 'Why would I need to make anything up? There's plenty of true stories to tell wee girls.'

'The orange man lives two doors down. He wears a bright-orange coat to go to his work. He collects cheeky wee children and puts them into his orange lorry. I'll leave what happens after that to your imagination.' Her eyes gleamed with excitement.

They looked like amber. I was petrified. Whenever I saw him after that day, I'd run inside. He gave me the creeps. In his truck he had two urban foxes that he had trained himself. They would never nip at the orange man, my grandmother said, but they would snap at the children. 'Fierce into their fingers!' He had trained the foxes to dislike kids. 'Can you imagine,' my grandmother said, 'being bitten by a fox?' I'd scream when I saw his bright-orange coat. I never saw him throw a child into his lorry. But once I saw him shut the doors very quickly. For all I knew, there might be some poor child in the back, struggling and screaming.

Another time I saw him walking along the railway line near Glasgow Queen Street station. We were on our way to visit my great aunt Peggy in Falkirk. Just near Bishopbriggs, I saw the orange man from the train window.

'Is that him?' I shouted.

'Who?' my grandmother asked.

'The orange man, of course!'

For some reason, which I still can't understand, she smiled. She smiled first, then she said, 'Oh, yes, that's him all right. Duck your head down, he might see you!'

Once I saw him on the Glasgow underground, on a train from Partick to Hillhead.

He looked as if he had grown taller. Then, later, he looked as if he had shrunk in the night.

My grandmother said the orange man could tell if a child was lying or naughty. He would take that child off in his orange lorry, and it didn't bear thinking about the next bit.

We were in her tenement flat and she had just made me eat up my bowl of sheep's stomach and potatoes and boiled cabbage before going to bed. She had made me swallow a teaspoon of cod-liver oil. She had made me drink my hot milk. She had made me brush my teeth. I did all this just in case the orange man would get me. I don't usually eat all my dinner or sit at the table. I don't usually eat haggis either. Yuk! It's horrible. It's nasty, but my grandmother likes it.

My mum usually lets me eat in front of the television. But my mum is doing her exams and I have to stay with my grandmother for a bit. My grandmother says she doesn't know what my mother is thinking about. 'Children these days are glued to the telly. In our day we didn't have a telly. We had to entertain ourselves.' My grandmother speaks first, then sucks her lips in tight. She shakes her head till it looks very wobbly.

I don't know what my mum thinks about

either. I think she thinks about me a lot because she loves me. She says, 'Who is my favourite girl in the whole wide world? Who loves you more than all the tea in China?' My grandmother says, 'You are spoilt rotten. Do you know that? Spoilt rotten. If I boil you an egg, you'll eat it, runny or not. We'll have less of the spoilt madam around here.' I don't know what she means.

Last night I slept in bed with my grandmother and she was very warm. Her bed is very high. I had to climb up into it. On the bottom of the bed were piles of old, yellowed newspapers with stories that went back for some time. I looked at the date on one of them: 12 July 1945. That was ages and ages before I was born. I was born on 17 June, seven years ago.

I woke up and wanted my mum. I wanted my mum's skin and her warmth. My grandmother shushed me to sleep. 'Quieten down,' she whispered. 'What do you think the orange man will do if he hears you are not sleeping?' Then a strange thing happened. It really happened. It happened to me.

In he came, the light was out. He was wearing his bright-orange coat. He had big black boots on his feet. He lifted me up and took me from the bed, and my grandmother didn't even wake up. She snored all the way through the theft of me. She snuggled in her covers while I was being stolen by the orange man. I was so frightened that my whole body felt empty inside. My heart was thumping like a wild rabbit's heart. He put me in the back of his truck and we travelled through my grandmother's streets in the very pitch-dark.

The orange light glowed from his big truck. The orange street lamps glowered. We passed the Royal Infirmary. We drove down towards Glasgow Cross. Then we drove over the bridge, crossing the river Clyde. We headed south. I know my directions. I've been good at directions since I was three. I thought, I must remember where I am going so that I can tell someone. *If* I get a chance to tell someone.

Soon, I was in the orange man's world. It wasn't a bit like my grandmother's description. Not at all. Not one bit. First of all there were foxes, but no foxes who bit my hand or snarled or snapped or barked in my face. No big black bags for smuggling children. No dustbin lorry. There were two lovely baby foxes. They needed to be fed. The orange man gave me a bottle, a real baby's bottle.

*

I fed the tiny one first. A she-fox. She had the darkest, deepest eyes. She was so cute, I could have taken her home to my room and introduced her to my dolls. Her little mouth sucked the bottle greedily. Then I fed the bigger one. He was the size of one of my dolls. 'Awwww,' I said. I *loved* the foxes. The orange man was staring at me. I jumped a little. Then I noticed that he was smiling, a really kind smile.

'Are you bad?' I plucked up the courage to ask him. 'Are you a bad man?'

'Oh, no!' He seemed very hurt. 'Not bad man, me,' he said. He didn't speak properly and he had a very strange voice, slippy and thick, but I could tell he was friendly. We stopped at a small house. He opened the door and I went in. 'I like orange. You like orange?' he asked.

I wondered if he would cry if I said no. But I said, 'Yes'. So he showed me all the orange things that he really loved. He opened a box and there was the most beautiful orange sunset. It floated in the room and a moon bobbed behind the clouds. Then it floated back. He gave me a clementine. I ate it. I was hungry. He made me mashed turnip with mashed carrot. It was very tasty. Then we had a bowl of pumpkin soup. Then a bowl of orange jelly. He asked me if I'd like marmalade for breakfast and I said I would have to go home. He gave me a big orange balloon which said 'Me Nice' on it. Then we got into his truck and he took me home. He wrapped an orange woolly blanket around me to keep me warm. The traffic lights changed from amber to green. The orange man put the truck into gear.

I could hardly believe it. In the morning, I woke up and told my grandmother what had happened. She said it was all a dream. She wouldn't believe me. She wouldn't believe that I had met the orange man and that the orange man was kind. 'Nobody steals children in the night. If somebody did that they would be a bad person, they wouldn't feed you. One of these days, Amy, your imagination is going to run away with you,' she warned me.

I imagined me and my imagination running across a big green field, hand in hand, screaming and laughing. I imagined us running across a yellow field. Then I imagined us running across an orange field. The orange one was best. The orange man was standing by the rowan tree. It was in full bloom. The birds were pecking at the berries. He had a big bowl in his hand. In the bowl were three orange fishes, swishing their tails.

The next day, my mum came to get me. 'That girl of yours has some imagination,' my grandmother said, her eyes twinkling. She was trying to pretend she was kind again. She liked doing that for my mum. 'Grandma tries to frighten me!' I told my mum.

'How?' she asked, looking worried.

'With her stories,' I said. 'Scary stories.'

'But they are only stories my mum said. 'And she's right. *You* are the one with the imagination.'

'I'm not,' I said. I don't know why I didn't

like it but I didn't. I think she was teasing me. 'Look!' I said, suddenly noticing that the orange balloon was in the car. It said 'Me Nice'. 'This proves he is real!'

'Who is real?' my mum asked.

'The orange man. He bought me this balloon and he took me to his orange house and let me feed his baby foxes in the middle of the night when Grandma was sleeping.'

'See what I mean? You and your imagination!'

'No! It's true. Look at this balloon!'

'That would be your grandma who bought you that,' my mum said smiling.

When we got home I went straight to the telephone. 'Can I phone Grandma?' I asked my mum. Then I carefully dialled the numbers. They were written down by the phone. When she answered, I asked her, 'Did you buy me an orange balloon that says "Me Nice" on it?'

'No. Not me. I hate balloons. Balloons frighten me. They burst when you're not expecting them to burst.'

'I told my mum it wasn't you,' I said.

'What?' she asked.

'Never mind.' I put the phone down. I was smiling. A huge big smile. They could call it what they liked. My imagination was real. I took a clementine out of the fruit bowl and peeled it for myself. I sang to myself, 'Oranges and lemons say the bells of St Clements.' Then I ate my clementine, segment by segment. It was sweet. It tasted orange. I wasn't going to be frightened by stories of the orange man ever again.

EACH TO THEIR OWN

Lindsey Fraser

Mum wanted to go abroad for the October half-term.

'It's too expensive,' Dad explained. 'Four flights, four hotel bills, four mouths to feed – it's just not on, love.'

'Well, neither is a wet week on the west coast.' Mum dumped a pile of ironing in Dad's lap, looked at him in her this-is-no-joke-Ken way, and swept out of the kitchen.

Dad looked at Robert and me. 'Tricky one this, boys,' he said.

Every day after that, Mum brought home holiday brochures by the kilo. 'Malta looks lovely,' she'd say, pretending she was just chatting. But we all knew perfectly well that she was deadly serious.

Sometimes Dad didn't say anything in reply, so we would try to fill the silences. 'Where's that?' we'd ask. 'Is it hot? Are there beaches. Can we take our Game Boys?'

Mum would pass us the brochure, saying, 'Give it to your father when you've had a look,' and then begin looking at the next one on her pile. 'Crete looks beautiful,' she'd say after a few minutes, and we'd have the same conversation all over again.

One evening Mum said, 'Ken, it's only four weeks until half-term.'

Dad looked at her with an especially sunny smile. 'Actually, I was going to talk to you about that, maybe after the boys have gone to bed?'

'It's our holiday too,' said Robert, grumpily.

'Bed, boys,' said Mum.

We were only half undressed when Mum came to hug us goodnight. *She* was the one smiling a big sunny smile now. 'Your dad is a genius,' she told us. 'A genuine genius.'

The next evening the reason for all that smiling became clear.

'To a *cottage*? With you? And Uncle Brian? And Molly and Kirsten?' Robert and I couldn't believe what we were hearing. 'And Mum's going off to Tenerife with Auntie Louise? On their *own*?'

'Yes,' said Dad.

'Without *us*?'

'Yes,' said Dad.

'Won't they be *lonely*?'

Dad turned to Mum. 'Will you be lonely, dear?' he asked.

'Of *course*,' she said. Her sunny smile was even sunnier – if that's possible.

Granny McCue drove Mum and Auntie Louise to the airport on half-term Friday and on the Saturday morning Dad's brother Uncle Brian arrived with our two cousins. The plan was to travel in convoy to the cottage. Dad had dragged all his camping equipment down from the loft – the stove, the billy cans, the folding cutlery, the plastic plates. Things were strewn all over the place.

'Running a little late?' suggested Uncle Brian.

'Just give us a hand to pack the bags, will you,' replied Dad.

Robert, Molly, Kirsten and I formed a human chain and after lots of to-ing and fro-ing, the boot of the car was packed. Dad slammed the lid shut and turned to us. 'You've got everything?' he asked.

Robert and I looked at each other.

'You know – clothes, wash stuff, a towel? Good grief – do I have to do everything for you?'

We ran first to the hall cupboard and grabbed a towel each, then to our chest of drawers and pulled out a bundle of clean clothes. Dad met us at the front door holding two carrier bags. 'Put all that in these,' he said. 'Now, let's get going.'

By the time we reached Fort William, Dad was on good form, singing along loudly to his favourite Proclaimers tape. Just as planned, we met Uncle Brian and the girls for a break. The dads were in a much better mood and we laughed like drains when Kirsten stuck a chip up each nostril. Nobody actually said it, but we knew that the mums would never have put up with that. The dads didn't seem to mind in the least.

It was getting dark by the time we drove into the village, and it was completely dark by the time we found the cottage. It felt as if we were driving round and round in circles but Dad said I was talking rubbish when I mentioned it and would I please put a sock in it.

He explained a little about the so-called cottage as he squinted into the gloom for anything resembling a signpost. 'Brian says it's quite basic – more of a *bothy* really, no kitchen or bathroom, but we've got everything we need. Your mother's always wittering on about air-fresheners and dry mattresses – we're made of sterner stuff than that, though, aren't we?'

We kept yelling, 'Yes!' in time to the bouncing of the car as it stotted over the potholes on the track leading to the cottage. When we finally saw it, we realized that Mum would most certainly not have liked it. The roof looked as if it might blow away in the next gust of wind.

Uncle Brian and the girls had arrived first. 'This is the life, Ken – no electricity, no hot water, just back to basics, the way holidays were in the old days.' We groaned. The girls were flashing their torches around or shining them under their chins, trying to look spooky.

'Get out your torches, boys,' ordered Dad, hauling a rucksack from the car.

There was a silence.

'Don't tell me . . .' he said, peering at our blank faces. 'Didn't I say to bring torches?'

'Actually, no,' I said. 'You didn't, or we would have.'

Dad sighed and shook his head. 'What would you do?' he said to Uncle Brian. 'I have to think of everything.' Uncle Brian winked at us behind Dad's back.

It was nearly nine o'clock by the time the cars were unpacked. Our stuff was dumped in the bigger of the two rooms, leaving Uncle Brian and the girls to the other one, the one with a squashy old mattress in it. There was a tiny hall between the two where we left our waterproofs.

In the main room there was a beaten-up old sofa on which the four of us huddled with our legs tucked up under the rug from Dad's car. We watched Uncle Brian as he tried to light the fire, but eventually he gave up on it, telling us that it was mild for October – we'd be fine and dandy.

Dad finally finished laying all his camping gear out in front of the fireplace and lit two candles. Uncle Brian put The Proclaimers on his portable CD player. Then, using an old camping tin-opener, they tackled the huge tin of ravioli they had brought for our tea.

Sweat was breaking out on Dad's forehead as he dug his way round the rim. 'I always remember this stuff from camping holidays in the old days,' he said through gritted teeth. 'Fabulous, warming and tasty. You're going to love it.'

'If we survive that long,' said Uncle Brian. 'I'm starving.'

And suddenly Robert and I realized how hungry we were and Kirsty and Molly began to haver about their empty tummies.

'Have you made your beds up?' Dad asked us sharply. 'Unroll those sleeping bags – give them a bit of an airing.' We didn't like to tell him that we'd done that already – the last time he'd asked. Eventually, after more grunting, there was a wet scwooshing noise and Dad folded back the tin lid in triumph. 'That'll do nicely,' he said, gazing at the lumpy tomato mixture in the tin. 'Now – have you got that camping stove going, Brian? No need for a saucepan,' he added as Molly tried to pass him one from the collection by the fireside, 'just makes for washing up, and none of us likes that, do we?'

The camping stove took another age. According to Uncle Brian, the matches were damp. According to Dad, Uncle Brian was a complete eejit. We just sat and giggled and yawned. The Proclaimers sang on. Theirs was the only CD we had and Uncle Brian had programmed the machine for continuous play.

I must have been dozing when Molly prodded me in the tummy and pointed to her watch.

10.40 p.m.

Ages past our bedtime.

We looked round at the others. Robert and Kirsten were asleep and our two dads were sitting on the floor, watching the large tin of ravioli on the tiny camping stove. Their faces looked grim in the flickering light of the blue gas flame.

'Dad?'

'Mmm . . .'

'There are some crisps in the car . . . should I go and get them? Just while we're waiting?'

'This'll only be a couple of minutes,' snapped Dad. 'Surely you can wait that long?'

'I think crisps are a great idea, Ewan, for our starters. Don't you think, Ken?' Uncle Brian turned to his brother.

Dad shrugged, never lifting his eyes from the tin of ravioli. 'Whatever,' he muttered.

The darkness outside was like a blanket – no street lights, no stars, no moon, no lights from the cottage. I groped around until I felt the bag of crisps, grabbed it, slammed the car door and ran back to the cottage. It must have been raining, I thought, because the ground was quite squelchy in places.

I was hardly in the room before Molly grabbed the crisps and ripped the bag open.

Within seconds it was empty. Kirsten even licked the insides. The crackling of the bag was the only sound apart from the gentle hissing of the stove and the faint singing from The Proclaimers. They were getting fainter because the battery was going flat – but I didn't like to say anything.

'Nearly there,' said Dad after a few minutes, 'it'll be bubbling in no time.'

Then Molly turned to me, scrumpled up her face in disgust and said, 'Phewwwww . . . you're absolutely *minging*!' And suddenly everybody was holding their noses, waving the air in front of their faces and glaring at me.

'I am not!' I yelled. But there was no doubt about it – a strong pong was coming from my direction or, more accurately, from my boots.

Uncle Brian leaned over and, holding a candle close, carefully lifted one of my feet off the floor. 'Let's have a look,' he said and then, almost immediately. 'Pwoooo . . . sorry, Ewan, but whatever it is, it's packed into the soles of your boots. Get them off and chuck them outside. We'll deal with them in the morning.'

I was furious. Wasn't I the one who had remembered the crisps in the car? Wasn't I the one who had bothered to go and get them? And now I was the one getting blamed for bringing a stink into the cottage. I stormed out of the room, pulled both boots off and threw them out through the front door. It was cold, I was starving, and I was tired. Some half-term holiday this was turning out to be.

At that moment there was a cry from next to the camping stove. 'It's boiling!' Dad yelled. 'Get your plates and let's eat!'

To be honest, the ravioli wasn't properly hot – everybody found some rather chilly little pasta parcels in their plateful. But we were so hungry that we didn't mind. In fact, we might have eaten more if there had been any, but there wasn't so we headed for our sleeping bags. Nobody mentioned washing up or brushing teeth. Uncle Brian held a torch so that we made it to the outside toilet and back without standing in anything smelly. Then we all snuggled down and silence fell. I vaguely remember Robert asking Dad what he'd brought for breakfast, but I don't think he got an answer.

I woke feeling very cold, but I wanted to get back to sleep so I wriggled further down into my sleeping bag and tried to force the chill out of my body. Dad was snoring gently. He was wearing his big Arran jumper and I thought he had his woolly hat on too – it was hard to tell. I heard Robert turn over and when he half-whispered, 'Ewan,' I poked my head up to find out what he wanted.

He was getting out of his sleeping bag. 'I'm going to block out that draught,' he whispered. 'It's Arctic over here.' He pushed the sleeping bag to his feet, scampered towards the door to the hallway, opened it and found himself face to face with a cow.

A black-and-white cow.

Robert let out an ear-splitting scream.

Black-and-white cows in fields with a

fence and even a car window between you and them are one thing. Black-and-white cows in your holiday cottage are quite another.

'Did you need to let that thing in here?' Dad asked groggily from the safety of his sleeping bag.

Uncle Brian appeared from his room at the other end of the cow with Molly and Kirsten peeking out from behind him. He looked a little puzzled and scratched his head, making his hair stand up even more than it already was. 'Someone can't have closed that front door last night.' Then he turned his attention back to the cow. 'But you are a splendid beast,' he said, and gave her a hearty wallop on the rump.

She clearly believed this to be an invitation to make herself even more at home. The cow walked a couple of steps further into our room, mooed loudly and then pooed at some considerable length.

The resulting cowpat steamed gently in the doorway.

Nobody spoke.

It was nearly lunchtime (although we hadn't had breakfast yet) before Robert stopped shaking. The crofter had come looking for the cow and explained that, having been hand-reared, the cow was always keen to make new friends. Molly and Kirsten had gone off with the cow and the crofter to collect eggs.

Robert and I couldn't go anywhere. The contents of our carrier bags had revealed two Cally Thistle football strips (long outgrown), two T-shirts, three pairs of swimming trunks, a pair of Mum's tights and a nightie that Dad said he'd never seen in his life. I expected him to be furious, but after a couple of deep sighs he started laughing.

'Good job this place isn't carpeted,' said Uncle Brian cheerfully, mopping madly to remove all evidence of the cow's visit. 'I've got a suggestion, Ken.' There was silence. 'Let's head for home. It's been fun. But let's face it, we're beaten.'

Dad held his hands up as though he were surrendering. 'Home. Warm bath. Comfy beds. Microwave oven. House-trained pets. No contest.'

So we spent the week going to Our Dynamic Earth in Edinburgh, the Glasgow Science Centre, Stirling Castle, Deep Sea World in North Queensferry and the Sea Bird Centre in North Berwick. We had fish and chips, not once but twice, and we enjoyed sleeping in our own beds.

Mum and Auntie Louise came home at the weekend looking healthy and relaxed.

'We had a ball,' we told Mum. 'Brilliant! You should have been there.'

At teatime Dad asked Mum if she had enjoyed her hot holiday.

'It was lovely, but actually, *secretly*, we were bored stiff. I kept wondering what you were up to. I felt I might be missing out.'

Dad gave her a hug. 'There's no pleasing some people.' He smiled at us across the top of her head. 'But it's true, you did miss out on quite a bit.'

THE TARTAN RAINBOW

Frank Rodgers

'Not many customers in today, Jimmy,' says Grandpa, wiping his hands on his white apron. He picks up the serving tongs and absent-mindedly rearranges the scones and apple slices on the counter.

I glance around at the empty chairs of the Cosy Café and nod. 'Not many yesterday or the day before, Grandpa,' I say.

'Aye, or last month or the month before. It's since those flashy new burger places opened.' Grandpa mutters this under his breath but I hear him anyway.

'Don't worry,' I say. 'Things will soon get better.'

Grandpa sighs, joins me at the window and we gaze out on to the darkening street.

He looks up at the sky and shakes his head. 'Typical Glasgow summer, eh, Jimmy? Sky so low and black I could poke my finger into the clouds and let the rain out.'

'Somebody's beaten you to it, Grandpa,' I say, pointing to the big drops beginning to hit the pavement.

'Typical,' he says again.

We're silent for a bit then out of the blue I say, 'Scotland played rubbish last night, didn't they?'

Grandpa gives a wheezing, rueful laugh. 'You've got a way of cheering a person up, Jimmy,' he says.

'Oh, I'm sorry, Grandpa. It just came into my head.'

He grins at me.

'Supporting Scotland is like supporting our local team, Partick Thistle,' he says. 'You just never know what they're going to do next. One minute they play like angels – like heroes – and the next like a bunch of dumplings.'

'So why do you support the Thistle, Grandpa?' I ask.

'It's a team for everybody,' replies Grandpa, 'no matter who you are. David and Goliath come into it as well,' he goes on with a grin. 'The Thistle are a wee team like Scotland is a wee country. So it's very satisfying to put one over on the big yins.'

'Like England,' I say, 'or Celtic and Rangers.'

He nods. 'Exactly.'

I stare out at the pelting rain. People scurry past trying to keep dry under umbrellas and newspapers. An old woman is wearing a plastic bag as a hat and two lads with number-one haircuts stroll past in T-shirts, laughing together as if the sun is splitting the trees.

'How come they want you to be like them?' I ask suddenly.

'Who?'

'Celtic and Rangers supporters.'

'Do they?'

'Well,' I reply, 'some of them do . . . two wee neds that live near me. One gives me a hard time because I don't support Celtic and the other does it because I don't support Rangers.'

Grandpa shakes his head. 'We can do without people like that,' he says. 'Just avoid them.'

'It's hard to, Grandpa,' I answer. 'They're always at me. And when they're not at me they're knocking lumps out of each other.'

Grandpa frowns. 'Have you been fighting?'

I don't want to worry him so I say, 'It's OK. I can look after myself.'

I get a long hard look from Grandpa and then he says, 'Take the heat out of it. Tell them you support Partick Thistle.'

'Tried that,' I say. 'Doesn't work with those two. Makes them laugh.'

'Wee . . .' Grandpa bites off what he was going to call them and turns away from the window. He steps up to the little fryer and opens the lid. The bubbly sound and lovely smell of frying chips fill the café. Grandpa lifts the basket of chips out of the crackling fat, props it on the fryer to drain and picks out a chip. Holding it between thumb and forefinger he gives it a squeeze and nods to me.

'Chips are ready,' he says. 'Fancy some?'

'Eating the profits, eh, Grandpa?' I say with a wink. It's something that Granny used to say and Grandpa smiles.

'Well,' he replies, 'no one else is eating them so we might as well.'

He fills two plates with chips and props the rest over the hot oil to keep them warm.

I can't wait and take one right away.

'Hoh!' I gasp, blowing past the hot chip in my mouth to cool it. 'Hoh . . . hoh . . . hoh!'

Just then two customers come in out of the rain.

Grandpa knows them and they call out, 'Hello, Alistair!'

'Aye, Sam . . . Agnes,' says Grandpa and nods and smiles.

As the couple collect their cups of tea and plates of chips Sam winks at me and says, 'Don't hang around in this country, son. Emigrate to Australia as soon as you're old enough. What me and Agnes should have done.'

Grandpa snorts. 'What's wrong with Scotland?' he says and Agnes grins.

'That,' she says, pointing at the rain outside. 'No summer, know what I mean?'

'Aye,' says Sam, taking a slurp of tea as he and his wife sit down. 'Billy Connolly got it right. There are two seasons in Scotland, he says. June and winter.'

He and Agnes snort into their teacups and Grandpa laughs.

'Fair enough,' he replies, 'but that's what makes the Scots tough.'

'You're not far wrong there, Alistair,' says Agnes, blowing on a chip.

Grandpa turns and begins to clean out the fryer, lifting out bits of batter and burnt chip with the strainer.

'Aye,' he murmurs, half to himself, 'we have to take the rough with the smooth.' He sees I am watching him and says, 'You can't go looking for a tartan rainbow.'

'A what?' I ask.

'A tartan rainbow,' he repeats. 'It's another of your granny's sayings. Her parents came to Scotland from Lithuania when times were hard there. When your granny was wee they told her that, for them, Scotland was like the pot of gold at the end of the rainbow. Your granny drew a picture of that rainbow and coloured it tartan. From then on she used to say you could find the answer to everything at the end of a tartan rainbow.'

'But there's no such thing,' I say.

'There you are, then,' replies Grandpa. 'We'll just have to make the best of things, won't we?'

Well, I try. And so does Grandpa.

But it's hard.

Next month Scotland loses at football again, it rains non-stop and the two wee neds seem to pick fights with me every second day.

Grandpa says his café will have to close if business doesn't pick up.

Then, one rainy day, something very strange happens. I'm walking to the café when it stops raining. (No, that's not the strange thing.) I look up. There's a bright patch of blue between the rain clouds and as I gaze at it a rainbow appears. It arcs out of the blue, past the grey clouds over the tops of the trees and seems to disappear on the other side of the old pavilion in the park.

I think I must be dreaming so I close my eyes then open them again. But it's still there. I can't believe it. It's a *tartan* rainbow.

I walk slowly in through the gates of the park. At the other end I see two kids on the swings. Their mother is pushing them one after the other and the kids screech with laughter. They haven't seen the rainbow.

I watch a man come into the park with his dog. He stops, looks in my direction then looks away again. He hasn't seen the rainbow either.

I look around the park. Rain drips from the climbing frame and the slide gleams like molten silver. It's like the world is going on without me.

Walking towards the pavilion I feel strange, like I'm walking in a trance. Everything around me seems normal – the black trees against the slatey sky, the sandy coloured tenements behind the park, the mottled green grass – everything normal . . . except for the tartan rainbow.

Treading carefully to avoid the piles of sodden leaves I move round to the side of the pavilion. It's full of shrubbery here and damp, earthy smells fill my nostrils. I can hear the dog barking somewhere in the background.

The end of the rainbow fades into one of the bushes. I stand beside it, not quite knowing what to do. Then, taking a deep breath, I peer under the bush. For a moment I can't see anything – it's dark under there – but suddenly I get a shock.

Surrounded by a faint tartan glow there's a smiling face looking back at me. A small, pale face with yellow eyes like a cat. The little chin has a fringe of red beard and is leaning on two thin, folded arms.

I just crouch and stare, my mouth open.

As my eyes become used to the lack of light I can see the face more clearly. It looks like a cross between a baby and an old man. The head is smooth, round and hairless, but there's a network of fine wrinkles around the eyes and mouth. The tip of the long nose quivers and, with a start, I realize that the ears are pointed.

A gnome? An elf? A fairy?

The yellow eyes blink and one of the small hands waves airily.

'You could say there's a bit of all three in me, Jimmy.' The voice is silvery – gurgly – like a river running over pebbles.

I'm stunned. He knows my name! He read my mind!

'It's quite easy to read minds,' the voice goes on. 'Humans are such transparent creatures.'

'Humans?' I gasp. 'So . . .'

The head nods. 'I'm a brownie,' he says. 'One of the last in Scotland.'

'I . . . I didn't know there were such things,' I stutter.

'You didn't know there were such things as tartan rainbows,' says the brownie, 'but there are. You just have to believe.'

'But I didn't know I believed,' I protest.

'Well, you do,' says the brownie. 'You're seeing me, aren't you?'

I nod.

'There you are then,' he says, sounding a bit like my grandfather. He peers up at me with narrowed eyes. 'Very well,' he snaps, his voice suddenly sharp. 'To business.'

'Business?'

'Aye,' says the brownie. 'Business. You have to give before you can receive.'

'Give what?' I ask.

The wrinkled face studies me for a moment.

'A home,' he says. 'A brownie needs a home and I am homeless.'

I'm startled and blurt out, 'But we've got no room in our house.'

The brownie frowns.

'I don't need a room,' he says. 'An attic or a cellar will do me fine. As long as there is a roof over my head I'm happy.'

My mind is whirling. How did I get into this conversation? What should I say? This doesn't feel real. Jumbled fragments of old tales and magic tumble through my head. I try to pin them down but can't catch any of them. Then suddenly they seem to fly together and make sense and the answer appears obvious.

'Yes,' I reply, and my voice startles me, sounding as if it's coming from a long way off. 'You can come and live in our attic.'

The brownie beams.

'Thank you,' he murmers, 'but I will not accept your offer.'

'What?' I ask, puzzled. 'Why not? I thought you said . . .'

'It was a test, you see,' says the brownie. 'Although I am indeed homeless I do not need a roof over my head. My task is to follow the rainbow and help those that find it help themselves. But first they have to pass a test. You have done that and now I can help you. So,' he says, peering at me intently, 'what is your hope?'

'Hope?' I say. 'Don't you mean wish?'

The brownie shakes his head.

'My powers in this modern world are sadly diminished,' he says. 'There was a time when I could grant wishes, but no more. Although,' he adds brightly, 'if you use my help well it can add to my power. All I can offer you at the moment is aid with one of your hopes. A *small* hope.'

'Well,' I respond immediately, 'this might be a big one but I hope Grandpa doesn't have to close his café. He loves it and it's all he's got since he lost Granny.'

The brownie smiles.

'You're a good lad, Jimmy,' he says. 'Unselfish. I like that. You've made me feel stronger already, do you know that? I usually only help people once but I might be able to do something extra for you later. *Might*, I say. So here's my response to your hope. Tell your grandpa to look in the envelope that lies in the bottom drawer of his wife's old cabinet. The one her parents brought to Scotland when they emigrated from Lithuania all those years ago. There's help there if he knows what to do with it.'

I'm not surprised any more that the brownie knows about such things so I nod. 'I will,' I reply.

'Very well,' says the brownie. 'Then I'll bid you goodbye.' He smiles at me and winks a yellow eye. 'Keep hope in your heart,' he says and vanishes.

I straighten up and look around me. The rainbow has gone too and the sun is shining in a clear blue sky.

Grandpa is setting out the cakes and biscuits on the counter when I arrive. He tries to look cheerful but I can see that he's worried about the café. I help him to get the place ready and serve the customers that come in over the next few hours. Once again there aren't many. The Cosy Café is dying on its feet.

All afternoon I wonder about telling Grandpa about the rainbow and the brownie. But I feel awkward and keep putting it off. Grandpa closes the café early and we set off towards his house. He has invited me for tea so we can watch the football on telly together. We pass the crowded, brightly lit burger place but Grandpa doesn't give it a glance. In step beside him I look up into his kind, worn face. There's something so friendly about walking together like this that I can't help myself and at last the story comes out in one big rush.

When I finish he stops walking and looks at me, not saying anything. Pulling out a hankie from his jacket pocket he blows his nose loudly then wipes the corner of an eye with the back of his hand.

'Aye,' he says softly. 'Your granny loved that old cabinet. When she died I couldn't bear to look at it. It made me too sad. I put it in the big cupboard in the hall. But now I'm going to bring it out again. It'll look nice in the front room.'

He doesn't mention the rainbow or the brownie. It's as if the only part of my story he heard was the bit about Granny's cabinet.

As soon as we are in the house I help Grandpa wrestle the cabinet into the front room. We place it next to the door and Grandpa smiles fondly as he looks at it.

'Nice,' he says, nodding, his thoughts far away. 'Lovely memories, Jimmy.'

After a moment he opens the bottom drawer, rummages among the bits and pieces there and takes out an envelope. Inside the envelope is a piece of folded paper. Grandpa smoothes it out and we both look at it.

'Is that Lithuanian, Grandpa?' I ask, pointing to the unfamiliar words.

He nods and a slow smile begins.

'It's a recipe,' he says.

'A recipe?'

'For *blynu*.' He pronounces it just like Granny used to: *blee-no*.

I blink in surprise. It's not what I expected. Somehow I imagined we might find something amazing like a treasure map, or a secret bank account . . . not a recipe for Lithuanian potato fritters!

Granny used to make them a lot and I can still remember the delicious taste, but why would the brownie think they could help Grandpa?

Before I can stop myself I say, disappointed, 'But what's the good of that?' Then it occurs to me. 'Unless . . .' I begin.

'Unless,' Grandpa goes on slowly, giving me a meaningful look, 'unless I try them out in the shop. Something new, home-made and delicious might tempt people back. It's worth a try. Give those shiny big burger places a dose of their own medicine, eh?' He looks at me and I see that some of the old sparkly Grandpa twinkle is back in his eyes. 'To the kitchen!' he cries.

It takes us most of the evening and we miss the football but it's worth it.

After three failed attempts – the first batch is too soggy, the second batch is burnt, the third batch is soggy on the inside and burnt on the outside – we make the perfect *blynu*.

It's absolutely delicious and we have two platefuls each.

Next day Grandpa puts a big sign in the window of the Cosy Café advertising the new delicacy and waits for the rush of customers. It doesn't happen. But the day after that, out of curiosity, two people try it out. Grandpa and I watch anxiously as they finish their meal. The couple smile and nod as they leave but don't say anything. Next day they come back with two friends and this time they tell us how much they like this new dish. The day after that Grandpa serves seven batches . . . the day after that ten . . . then seventeen . . . twenty. People on the street are beginning to talk about the lovely new grub down at the Cosy Café. They come in and ask about it. They taste it and love it. They tell their friends, their families, their cousins, aunties and uncles about it, and soon everyone knows. The Cosy Cafe becomes one of the most successful cafés in Glasgow. It's always full. Sometimes there are even queues. Grandpa gets a new lease of life, opens other Cosy Cafés all over the city and every one of them is full of people eating the most popular food in town. *Blynu* . . . made to a secret, Lithuanian recipe with fresh, Scottish ingredients. *Blynu* with everything! *Blynu* with egg, *blynu* with sausage,

blynu with ham, *blynu* with roast vegetables, *blynu* with *blynu*!

The burger places are worried.

It's wonderful to see Grandpa back to his old self again.

I'm feeling better too, and it's nothing to do with the weather. That's still the usual mix of rain and clouds with a dash of sun. No, it's to do with the two wee neds. They've stopped tormenting me and fighting with each other since the miracle. You see, one morning they woke up and realized they were Partick Thistle supporters. Was this the 'extra' thing the brownie said he might do for me? I tell this to Grandpa and he roars and laughs.

'Wonderful!' he cries. 'Tell them there's a free plate of *blynu* waiting for them at the Cosy Café whenever they like.' He looks at me and winks. 'You know what this means, Jimmy,' he says, his eyes twinkling. 'It means that anything is possible. *Anything*!'

I wink right back and grin.

'You're right, Grandpa,' I say. 'It means that we can keep on hoping that one day . . . one day . . . Scotland will win the World Cup!'

BIG BRUCE

Vivian French

Who's Big Bruce? He's my gran's cat. He's HUGE. His fur is thick and black, and his paws are like big fat pincushions, and he weighs a ton. He's old, too, and he spends most of his time asleep on my gran's bed . . . but sometimes he has to go out. You can guess why. And he's so old and fat that he finds the tenement stairs up to Gran's flat very hard work. He puffs as he goes down, and he wheezes on the way up, so he has to be carried. Sometimes he thinks he'll not bother with all those stairs and he goes into the kitchen and *whoops*! There's this *horrible* smell, and Gran goes mad. That's why he has to be taken out, even if he doesn't want to go. When Gran's on her own she takes him first thing before she goes to work, but when me and Bonny are staying we have to take him downstairs after we've had our breakfast. All the way down, shut the main door so's he can't sneak back in, put him outside on the drying green and wait until . . . well, until he's done what he's supposed to. Even if it's raining.

ESPECIALLY when it's raining.

Big Bruce hates rain. When it's sunny he's

not too bad, but if there's even a dribble of a drizzle he knows. He disappears. You wouldn't think there'd be that many places to hide in my gran's wee flat, but there are. Gran knows all his hidey holes, but we don't, so Gran leaves us with a tin of sardines. Big Bruce hates rain, but he *loves* sardines – and he's greedy. Very greedy. If there's a sardine about, Big Bruce wants it. He comes gallumphing out from wherever he's been hiding – and we grab him. He doesn't try to get away; as soon as anybody picks him up his bones sort of melt, and he turns into a giant, furry pyjama bag until you put him down again. He's cunning, though; Bonny once made the mistake of putting him down on the landing outside Gran's flat before I'd shut the door, and Big Bruce was away back inside in a flash – and straight into the kitchen.

POOH!

You will *not* want to know what he did, but even Mrs MacSplinter could smell it. She came hurrying out, and I suppose it was a good thing really because by the time Gran got back at lunchtime all you could smell was disinfectant. (By the way, if you're worrying that Gran left us alone in the flat while she went to work, she didn't. Mrs MacSplinter lives next door, and she kept her front door open all the time Gran was away, and she popped in and out on us.)

It was a rainy Friday when Bonny had her bright idea. It'd been raining all week, and we were fed up with Big Bruce. He was fed up with us too. We'd been heaving him up and down the stairs for days. It took us ages to catch him in the mornings, and he'd taken to rushing under a nearby bush when we finally parcelled him out of the main door. Then he'd not do what he was meant to do for hours. Once, he'd taken so long that Gran had come back from work and found us still hanging about waiting for him.

'The wee rascal!' she'd said. 'Maybe you should just bring him down here and leave him. You can fetch him back later.' That was better, but it meant we had to traipse up and down the stairs twice as often – and there were ninety-five steps. Bonny counted them. Her legs were shorter than mine and she noticed them more than I did.

Anyway, Bonny had this idea. We'd been messing about in Gran's hall cupboard the night before and we'd found this big old shopping basket. We left it out, and in the morning it was still there – with Big Bruce inside it. Quite a lot of him bulged over the edge, but he didn't care. He was fast asleep. Bonny saw him, and she came rushing into the kitchen where I was eating cornflakes.

'Calum!' she said. 'I know just how we can let Big Bruce out – and we'll not need to go down the stairs at all. He's in Gran's basket. We can tie the basket to a rope and lower him out the window!'

I wasn't too sure at first, but Bonny sorted it all. She found Gran's old washing line and tied it, with lots of knots, to the handle of the basket. Big Bruce didn't even stir. Then she opened the kitchen window. It took the two of us to carry the basket in from the hall, but that cat didn't even flicker an eyelid. Bonny held the rope tightly, I lifted the basket up to the window . . . and lowered it over the sill.

It worked!

Big Bruce, still fast asleep, swung peacefully in mid-air. Bonny began to let the rope out, and the basket slowly descended. I watched as the basket dropped down and down, almost halfway to the ground.

'Bonny,' I said, 'you're a genius.' And at exactly that moment Big Bruce woke up. He yawned. And stretched. And jumped out of the basket – and vanished.

I gawped. Bonny clutched my arm. 'Look!' she said. 'There's a ledge. He must have jumped through someone's window.' We stared down in horror, and as we did so there was a loud *crash*! from below.

Bonny turned pale. 'Oh, no,' she said. 'Big Bruce is smashing up the china in some poor person's flat!'

Something exploded in my head. 'Quick!' I yelled, and I grabbed the rope and began to haul the basket up as fast as I could. 'Get the sardines, Bonny – we've got to get him back!'

Bonny dashed off to the fridge and came back with the open tin. I scooped the sardines into the basket and then I lowered it out of the window until it was back outside the ledge where Big Bruce had vanished. The basket swayed a bit in the wind, but we did our best to keep it as still as we could.

'Brucie,' Bonny hung out of the kitchen window as far as she could. 'Puss, puss, puss. Come and get your sardines!'

There was no answer.

I tried. 'Puss, puss, puss? Big Bruce.'

Nothing happened.

'It's no good,' Bonny said. 'He didn't like it in the basket. That's why he—' She stopped dead. We both held our breath.

Something large and black and furry was crouched on the window ledge of the flat below. Something large and black and furry was patting at the basket. Something large and black and furry was – *yes* – stepping inside!

'Slowly!' I breathed, and little by little we edged the basket upwards. Big Bruce was far too busy with the sardines to notice what was going on. Bonny reached out to bring it back into the safety of the kitchen. 'Got him!' she squeaked triumphantly, and heaved the basket on to the kitchen worktop. 'Come on out, Big – oh!'

For the second time that morning our eyes popped out on stalks as we stared.

It wasn't Big Bruce.

It was a completely strange cat – just as

big and as black as Bruce, but with round green eyes and a torn ear. He sat up in the basket, licked his lips, looked at us and purred loudly.

'Oh no!' Bonny said, which was exactly what I was thinking. But then she leaned forward and tickled the cat's ears. He purred even louder, jumped down to the floor and began to rub his back against Bonny's legs.

'He's lovely,' Bonny said.

'Yes,' I said, 'but what are we going to do? Big Bruce is smashing up the flat down below, and now we've catnapped their pet pussy. Whoever lives there isn't going to be very happy.'

Bonny didn't seem to take any of this in. She was sitting on the floor with the cat in her lap. 'Couldn't we just keep him?' she said. 'It's a fair swap.'

'No!' I said. 'Gran would be furious. We've got to put him back. And get Big Bruce back, too, before he does any more damage.'

Bonny began to giggle. 'Perhaps they were having a china-throwing party!'

I glared at her. How could she think it was funny? 'When they find out we'll be grounded for weeks,' I said fiercely. 'Put it back in the basket.'

Bonny looked suddenly serious. She tried to pick up the huge purring cat, and *whoooooooosh*! He was gone. Out of the kitchen, through the hall – and into Gran's room. With one mighty spring and a cloud of dust he zoomed up in the air and on to the top of Gran's wardrobe. He skidded to a stop, turned round twice, and sat down.

I looked at Bonny. Bonny looked at me. 'Now what?' she said.

I stared at the cat. He stared back. He was fluffed up like a monstrous black puffball, and his green eyes glinted.

'Shut him in here for now,' I said. 'We've got to get Big Bruce back. But we've got to hurry – Gran'll be back soon.' I didn't want even to think about what Gran would say if she found a strange cat camping out on top of her wardrobe *and* Big Bruce missing.

Back into the kitchen we went, shutting Gran's door behind us. We hunted in the cupboard for more sardines but there were none left.

'The basket still stinks of them,' I said, and it was true. 'Just put it out, and we'll hope for the best.'

We slung the basket out of the window again. It had stopped raining, but the wind was still blowing and the basket twirled round and round as we dropped it down.

'Big Bruce'll never get into that,' Bonny said.

'Try and land it on the window ledge,' I said. 'If we swing it out and then back it should work.'

Bonny twitched the rope, but the basket just twirled faster.

'Let me do it.' I climbed up on to the worktop and leaned out of the window as far as I dared. Bonny clutched at my legs, but I couldn't fall out because Gran had this safety bar thing in the way. I held on to the bar with one hand and swung the rope as hard as I could . . . and the basket flew away from the wall and back towards the open window . . .

. . . just as Big Bruce appeared on the ledge. I made a horrified gurgling noise as the swinging basket scooped Big Bruce up. He let out a massive *merrrrowl*! and hung on with all his claws. 'Argggh!' I screeched as his massive weight wrenched my arm. Big Bruce flew downwards. Zoooooom . . .

. . . Bonny grabbed the rope, and the basket stopped with a jolt about half a metre above the ground. Big Bruce scrambled out, and he looked just fine – well, maybe a bit fluffed up and offended. He stalked away across the drying green and then stopped, and did what he was meant to do.

'I'll go and get him!' Bonny said, and she shot off out of the flat and down the stairs. I hauled up the rope and the basket and stuffed it at the very back of the hall cupboard. I was just wiping some of the sardine oil and footprints off the worktop when I heard Bonny coming back, so I went to open the front door. But it wasn't Bonny. It was Gran.

I started to say, 'Oh no!' and had to change it into a 'Hello!' Luckily Gran wasn't alone, so she didn't notice anything. She was with a tall boy and I vaguely recognized him as someone who lived in the building. His face was screwed up with worry, and he was carrying two milk cartons.

'Calum, this is David,' Gran said as she swept us all through to the kitchen. 'He was wondering if you'd seen his cat. He says he left the window open when he went to get some milk, and he thinks Moggie must have jumped out.'

The boy groaned. 'Mam'll kill me. She's

forever telling me to shut the windows – but
Moggie's never jumped out before.' He
looked even more miserable. 'And he's
knocked over Mam's best vase.'

'That'll be what scared the poor wee
beastie,' Gran said. 'But I'm sure he'll be
fine. Calum and Bonny'll help you look,
won't you?' And she took off her coat and
slung it over a chair – and that's when I had
my brilliant idea.

'I'll put your coat in your room, Gran,' I
said.

Gran looked a bit surprised. 'Thank you,
dear,' she said.

I snatched up the coat and charged across
the hall and then, very carefully, opened
Gran's bedroom door. My eyes swivelled to
the top of the wardrobe – no cat.

I stared round, and there he was.

Big black Moggie – fast asleep in the
middle of Gran's bed.

Quick as a flash, I threw Gran's coat on
top of him and scooped up the squirming
bundle. I shot to the front door in a flurry of
fur, claws and coat, and rushed outside. By
the time I'd got to the top of the stairs,
Moggie was free – and Gran and David
came out of the kitchen just in time to see
Bonny puffing up the stairs, Big Bruce in her
arms, and in front of her – streaking back

into our flat – Moggie.

'Moggie!' yelled David, and dropped the milk all over the floor.

Which was just as well, because otherwise Gran might have asked some awkward questions about why I was *outside* the flat with her coat . . . and why it was covered with dusty paw prints.

We never did own up. We talked about it but, as Bonny said, we couldn't be *absolutely* certain that it was Big Bruce who broke the vase. I mean, Moggie was in the flat when it happened. And David told us later that his mum wasn't as mad about it as he'd thought she would be. Apparently it had belonged to some old aunt, and she'd never been that keen on it.

And another thing. Big Bruce always asks to go out now. He stands at the flat door and miaows. Even if it's raining.

THE LAST BOX

Theresa Breslin

'Aarghhhh!'

Morven Cardross hurriedly closed her lunch bag and looked around the school dinner hall. The infants were finishing up, and the juniors had just begun lunch. Thank goodness no one had heard her apart from the two friends sitting opposite.

'What's wrong?' asked Shona Hamilton.

Morven cautiously opened her lunch bag again and pointed dramatically to the contents. 'Mouldy tomatoes!' she announced. 'Monday morning, and I've got mouldy tomatoes! Dad said he would make me a packed lunch today and he's forgotten. This is Friday's leftovers.'

Josh McKinnon, who was sitting opposite Morven, peered across the table. 'Yuck!' he said.

He prised open the lid of his own plastic container. Morven saw that he had a packet of crisps, a round red apple, and three, freshly made, diagonally cut, cucumber sandwiches. A small sprig of parsley lay neatly on top.

'I'm fed up with Dad forgetting about my lunches,' Morven said. 'I wish *I* had a Mum to make me sandwiches like yours.'

'Ha!' snorted Josh. 'You must be joking! I do my own. My mum is so scatty that she'd probably spread my bread with rabbit droppings. Last night she put the baby out on the front door step, and the milk bottles in the bath.' He opened his crisps and offered the packet to Shona and Morven.

'The baby outside, and the milk bottles in the bath?' repeated Shona. 'She didn't! I don't believe you.'

'Believe me,' said Josh. 'She did.'

It was probably true, thought Morven. Everyone knew that Josh's mum was an eccentric artist who was always getting things mixed up, whereas she, Morven, had managed to keep it fairly quiet from the rest of the class about her dad being a bit dreamy and forgetful. Morven looked down at the damp tomato blobs stuck among the crumbs of last Friday's lunch. If anyone saw this she'd soon be known as the Saddo Sandwich Girl.

'There should be a special allowance for children like us,' she said seriously to Josh. 'It's all too much for us to cope with.'

'Too much,' Josh agreed between mouthfuls of cucumber sandwich.

Near home time, when their teacher, bossy Mr Pritchett, reminded the class about the local Highland Games, Morven thought again about her dad. 'Please bring in donations for the school stall,' Mr Pritchett said. 'Home-baking, craftwork, contributions for the white elephant table. But especially this year I need adult participation. Our class will be demonstrating games, traditional and new. A "Pastimes of Past Times and New Age" sort of thing. I'm planning hopscotch and races with girds and cleeks. I want to see dancing displays, and games with marbles and skipping ropes side by side with skateboarding. Everyone must wear a pair of wellies, and when they have the traditional tossing the caber, we'll have a Great Welly Boot throwing competition. You must nag your parent or carer to come along next Sunday and take part.'

My dad will forget to turn up, thought Morven. 'Mr Pritchett,' she began, 'my dad won't . . .'

Josh recalled his mum's last attempts at home-baking: the sad little scones, the exploding rock cakes. 'Mr Pritchett,' he said. 'My mum can't . . .'

Their teacher put his hands over his ears. 'I can't hear *can't* and I won't hear *won't*,' he said. 'No negatives – *Pritchett thinks Positive*.' He waved a sheet of paper in the air and beamed at the class. 'You will all take this form home with you. On it is a list of duties for the day with a box to tick beside each duty, *and* it's in its own envelope, so that you don't lose it among all the other bits of paper in your schoolbags. Your parent, carer, auntie, big brother, dog or hamster need only tick *one* box. Just do it,' he ordered. 'Get them to sign up tonight.'

'But . . .' said Josh.

'But . . .' said Morven.

'But me no buts,' said Mr Pritchett firmly. 'I expect a representative from every household.' He handed each pupil an envelope just as the final bell rang. 'Filled in, signed and returned. Tomorrow, or else.'

Morven and Josh looked across the classroom at each other and shook their heads. Josh chewed the end of his pencil in despair. To involve his mum would mean disaster. She always did things back to front. Last Christmas she had helped make costumes for the school play and all the ones she had sewn fell apart during the performance. They found out later that she had threaded the sewing machine in reverse. Josh's own costume had unravelled as he strode across the stage. He was meant to be the King of Winter banishing the Flowers of Summer. After crashing a huge pair of cymbals together, he had commanded the shivering Flowers in a loud voice to, 'Wither and Die in the Cold Darkness.' But the dramatic impact was completely ruined when he tripped on the trailing hem of his icicle cloak, fell flat on his face and banged his head on one of the cymbals. Josh spat out pencil-wood splinters and crushed Mr Pritchett's envelope down into his rucksack as he got up to leave. He wouldn't even bother looking at the list. There wouldn't be anything that his mum could do.

Morven opened the envelope and stared at the piece of paper. Beside her Shona was already choosing boxes where her parents could help out. Morven squinted sideways.

Right at the top Shona had skipped 'line dancing' but had ticked almost every other box. Further down, in the blank space for additional ideas, Shona had written that her mum could bring her spinning wheel and do a demonstration. Morven sighed. There would be nothing that her dozy dad would be able to cope with. He was a children's writer and spent a lot of time in the other world of his imagination. Frequently she found him wandering about the house trying out dialogue for his books, or having conversations with the cat. It was *she* who had to remind him to shop, feed the poor cat, pay the TV licence, organize dinner and do all the other everyday things. Morven's eye ran down the page. No way could he play hopscotch or marbles. It was a lost cause. Then she saw the very last box. She grinned.

'Josh!' she shouted as she saw him going out through the school gates with his friends. 'The last box!' Morven called. 'For your mum,' she explained, waving Mr Pritchett's form in the air. 'For the Highland Games. Try the last box!'

The last box.

Josh remembered Morven's words later that night as he was about to go to bed. His mum was painting at her easel in the back bedroom while the baby crawled among old newspapers spread out on the floor.

'Look at this, Josh,' his mum frowned. 'This tree is not quite the right green, and I don't know why. Do you think the tint is too deep?'

Josh glanced at the painting. It was blazing with brightness, just like their house in which every inside door was painted a different colour. Orange and ochre, azure and lime, red and yellow. He stuck the form under his mum's nose. 'Mr Pritchett says that an adult from each household has to be there,' he said. 'It's for the Highland Games next week. The school has a stall and is running events and everyone has to do something.'

'Oh, goody!' said his mum. 'I love the Highland Games.' She signed the form and then hesitated before giving it back to him. 'I thought you said that, after the Christmas show, I wasn't allowed to help with anything at the school ever again.'

'Mr Pritchett said every parent had to be there,' said Josh. 'He's put a box at the end for those that are not good at anythi . . . at games. He wants volunteers to keep the children in line while they are waiting to take part. Even you should manage that.'

The baby made a grab for a tube of red paint. Josh made a grab for the baby. Josh's mother ticked the box, put the form in the envelope, sealed it, and gave it back to him.

When Morven got home, her dad was kneeling by the fire, talking to the cat. The cat was sitting very still in the armchair.

'How does that sound?' her dad was asking the cat.

'Dad,' said Morven.

'What if . . . I changed the fairy tale around,' said Morven's dad, 'and Goldilocks was actually a Breakfast Burglar? Supposing . . . people's breakfasts had been going missing for ages, and no one knew why. Just imagine . . . if you made your toast and laid it on the table all hot and buttery, turned round to get the teapot, turned back, and Fwoot! It was gone.'

The cat carefully licked a paw.

'Da-ad!' cried Morven. She lifted the cat, who had a slightly stunned expression on its face, and sat down on the chair.

'Oh,' Morven's dad blinked a couple of times. 'It's you, dear.' He blinked again. 'I was trying a story idea out on the cat. She seemed to like it.'

'Listen, Dad,' said Morven. 'Mr Pritchett needs help for the school display at the

Highland Games next week. Do you think you could concentrate long enough to keep children in line while they wait for their turn at the games?'

Her dad thought hard for a moment. 'You know, I think I might be able to do that.' He smiled happily. 'I could tell them stories.'

'Right,' said Morven. She handed her dad the envelope. 'Sign this form and tick the box at the end.' She sniffed the air. 'What's that burning smell? Is there something cooking?'

'Potatoes?' asked her dad.

'When did you put them on to boil?' demanded Morven.

'Emmm . . .' said her dad.

Morven leaped to her feet and ran into the kitchen to rescue the potatoes. Her dad ticked the box, sealed the envelope, and put it back into Morven's schoolbag.

She should have checked the form. Morven realized that the next weekend as soon as the Highland Games began. It was just like her dad to misread the information. The piper had stopped playing, the opening ceremony was over, and they were all standing at the space on the grass next to the school stall when Mr Pritchett said, 'Right, now that the welly boot throwing is under way, let's get the rest of our events started. Shona ask your mum to set up her spinning wheel here, please.' He turned to Josh and Morven, 'You could bring your mum and dad to begin the line dancing now.'

Morven turned pale. Her dad had just done his welly boot throw and she'd been about to help him get the rest of the competitors in line.

'The what?' said Josh in a tight panicky voice. 'My mum didn't put her name down for line dancing.' He paused. 'Did she?'

'Yup,' said Mr Pritchett. He consulted his clipboard and waved to Josh's mum and Morven's dad to come over. 'They've both marked the first box and signed on the bottom.'

'The *last* box!' said Morven and Josh together.

'Nope,' said Mr Pritchett. 'Top box ticked for both of you. Line dancing. Here. Now.'

'Am I doing line dancing?' said Josh's mum. 'I'm not sure that I can—'

'Of course you can,' said Mr Pritchett briskly. 'Just get it started, please.'

'Oh, well.' Josh's mum laughed and thrust the baby into Mr Pritchett's arms. She began to clap her hands and stamp her feet. 'Come on, everybody! One. And Two. Forward. Back. And, er . . . one, two, three!'

Morven's dad and a few younger children lined up behind her and began to copy her movements.

'This is quite easy really, once you get started,' said Josh's mum as she dipped and swayed and slapped her knees.

The baby dribbled on Mr Pritchett's fleece jacket. Josh and Morven edged away from the scene.

'Yee-ha!' shouted Josh's mum. 'Should I twirl around now?' she asked no one in particular.

'Turn left, I think,' suggested Morven's dad helpfully.

Which, if she had done, just *might* have been almost all right, thought Josh. But in his mum's mind, 'left' meant 'right'.

Clicking her fingers in full, high-stepping mode and followed by her loyal little group, Josh's mum spun right, cannoned against Shona's mum, knocked her spinning spinning wheel sideways, and fell right into the welly boot competition.

Josh covered his eyes.

Josh's mum sat in the middle of the pile of welly boots. She picked one up. 'This is the *exact* colour of green I want for my painting.' She waved the boot in the air. 'Who owns this welly boot?'

'It's mine actually,' said Morven's dad,

getting out from under the spinning
spinning wheel.

'You have wonderful taste in wellingtons,'
said Josh's mum.

'I never think of them as wellingtons,' said
Morven's dad. 'More like seven-league
boots. For a giant,' he added, as Josh's mum
gave him a blank look.

'What an amazing imagination!' said
Josh's mum. 'May I borrow your boot to
match a colour shade for my painting?'

'Of course you may,' said Morven's dad,
helping her to her feet.

'How do you know about seven-league
boots?' asked Josh's mum, tucking the welly

boot snugly into the crook of her arm.

'Oh, I do research for my stories,' said Morven's dad.

'Stories?' said Josh's mum.

'Yes,' said Morven's dad. 'Would you like to hear one?'

Morven and Josh watched as his mum and her dad wandered off among the crowds. Morven's dad was hobbling a little on account of wearing only one welly boot.

'Could have been worse, I suppose,' said Morven.

'A lot,' agreed Josh.

He could see that his mum's skirt was outside in. But Morven's dad hadn't noticed, and anyway the skirt material had so many splodges of coloured paint on it that you would hardly know that it was the wrong way round. A bit like my house, Josh thought. Even though things were often topsy-turvy, having so much bright colour around kind of made up for it. It's like being inside a rainbow, one of his friends had said. Josh thought about that. He decided that he liked living in a rainbow.

Morven saw that her dad was chatting away but, unlike the cat, Josh's mum was paying close attention. Morven knew that her own favourite time of day was when, each night before she went to bed, her dad made time to talk to her, and began sentences with, 'What if . . .' or 'Just imagine . . .' or 'Supposing . . .'

'Look at her,' said Josh. His mum had hefted Morven's dad's welly boot over her shoulder and was patting it gently. 'She's trying to burp your dad's welly boot. I'd better collect our baby from Mr Pritchett.'

'Let's leave them for a bit. Serve him right for being so bossy,' said Morven. 'Fancy an ice cream?'

PORRIDGE AND ME

Janet Paisley

Before Porridge, there was me and my dad and my dog, Scruff. Scruff is wee and white and stumpy. My dad says dogs can't laugh. But Scruff grins all the time. He sleeps at the bottom of my bed and watches at the window for me coming home from school. When he sees me, he grins and turns round and round in circles, wagging his stumpy tail. He's my very best friend.

'I've been thinking,' my dad said one day. Thinking is not my dad's best thing. He doesn't do it very often. When he does, it's always a bad idea. 'You could do with a brother,' he said.

This time he'd flipped. Gone doolally. I mean, what could any girl *do* with a brother? And where did he think we'd get one? You can't just nip down to the BROTHER shop and buy one. Before you get a brother, you need to get a mother. We didn't have one of those. Wouldn't you know, my dad had thought of that too.

'A ready-made brother,' he said. 'Your size. I'm going to marry his mother.'

When your dad says something like that, you can do three things. One, say nothing.

Two, pretend you didn't hear. Three, go to your room and play shoot 'em up. Whatever you do, don't try screaming. Or turning white and falling over. Or being sick, lots of times, all over the sofa and the rug. It doesn't work. I tried them all.

'Stop mucking about, you,' my dad said.

Scruff put his head on his paws and blinked up at me with big sad eyes. Things couldn't get worse, could they?

My new brother Porridge was worse. He had spiky hair. His jumper was on back to front. His socks didn't match. Dad left us alone to *get to know each other*.

'And behave,' he said before he went.

'Your jumper's on back to front,' I said, nicely.

'How do you know?' Porridge asked.

'See that label?' I poked his chest, 'it goes at the back, dopey.'

THUMP! He whacked me.

'Do that again and I'll tell on you.'

THUMP! He skelped me again.

'Da-a-ad!'

THUMP! He kicked me.

'Stop mucking about, you two,' my dad shouted up from downstairs. Us *two*?

Scruff licked my face and growled at Porridge. He was a lumpy, loony gowk, not a brother. Things couldn't get worse, could they? His mum was something else. The woman was *house*-sized. HUGE.

'Meet Tina,' my dad said. The living room went dark when she stood up. I peered up through the gloom. Up and up and up till I had a crick in my neck. Tina's head touched the ceiling. She had arms like punchbags and fingers like pink pork sausages. The sofa disappeared under her when she sat down. She was so wide it would take a week to walk round her. My dad was going to marry a mountain.

'Well, what do you think?' my dad asked, smiling at her.

'We can do sponsored walks round her,' I said.

'Stop mucking about,' he said, laughing.

Tina rumbled like thunder. When she rumbled, she shook. When she shook, the whole house shook too. All the ornaments fell off the shelves. She wasn't just a mountain. She was a *volcano*.

'Oh, you are funny,' she rumbled. 'Sponsored walks. Don't make me laugh.'

'I love it when you laugh,' my dad said. Flipped, like I said. Gone doolally.

The house was full now. One room was always full of Tina. The spare room was full of Porridge. Scruff and me started going for lots of walks, just to keep out of the way. Things couldn't get worse, could they?

I was putting Scruff's lead on.

'I think you should take Porridge with you,' Dad said. See what I mean about him and thinking? They just don't go together.

'Can't,' I said. 'I've only got one lead.'

'What d'you want another lead for?' Porridge said.

See, the thing about Porridge is, he's thick. Not thick like the soles of my trainers. Not thick like syrup. Thick like when I made a joke and he just looks. Porridge just doesn't get it. Not ever.

'To walk you as well,' I told him.

THUMP!

'Stop mucking about, you two,' my dad said.

'Oh, you're a right pair,' Tina Volcano rumbled. The cupboards in the kitchen started to rattle on the walls. I got out quick. Porridge got out right behind me.

'If you follow me, I'll thump *you*,' I said.

'You and whose army?'

But my dad wasn't around now. I didn't have to behave. THUMP!

'I'm telling on you,' he said.

THUMP!

'Mu-u-um!' he yelled.

THUMP! I whacked him some more.

'Who wants to come with you anyway,' Porridge said. 'Call that a dog? Hairbrush on a string, more like.'

Scruff started to bark.

'Call that a bark?' Porridge said. 'Yip, yip, yip.'

Scruff bit his ankle.

'Aoww!' Porridge yelled, hopping about holding his ankle. 'I'll get that dog. You wait. I'll get him. You wait and see!'

Scruff and me went down the canal. He likes it down there. There aren't any cars so he can come off the lead. He runs up and down the towpath. Sometimes he runs to the water and I shout 'Stop!' So he skids to a stop just before he goes over the edge, grins at me and wags his tail. Like he's making a joke. Kidding on he's going to jump in.

I bent down and scratched behind his ears. 'I'm glad you bit him.'

Scruff jumped up and licked my face. Now we had to live with a lumpy thicko and a volcano. And I was just one of *you two*. Things couldn't get worse, could they?

Two days later, Scruff was gone. He wasn't looking out of the window when I came home from school. He didn't run to the door when I came in. He wasn't hiding under the bed, waiting to pounce on my feet. He wasn't anywhere.

'I never touched your stupid dog,' Porridge said.

'He must've slipped out,' the Volcano growled. 'Aw, never mind, he'll come back.' She stood up. Everything went dark. She bent over me and her punchbag arms opened as if she was going to grab and squeeze me. They'd got rid of Scruff. Now they were going to get rid of me. I ran for it.

I didn't stop running till I was safe down the canal. I sat on the edge and stared at the mucky water. What had they done to Scruff?

'He won't be in there,' a voice said behind me. 'That water's manky.' It was Porridge. I glared at him. 'Hey,' he said. 'Are you crying?'

'Course I'm not crying.' I jumped up and got ready to thump him. 'My eyes are watering, that's all. What do you think I am, a girl?'

'Well, yes,' he said.

See what I mean about thick?

THUMP! I whacked him.

'Aoww!' he yelled. 'I didn't mean a cry-baby girl. I meant a girl girl. And if you thump me again, I won't help look for your stupid dog.'

I nearly thumped him again for saying Scruff was stupid. But I was glad he was there. Two people looking was better than one. Even if one of them did have his jumper on back to front. I could always thump him after we found Scruff. If we didn't find Scruff, I'd thump him anyway.

'I'll go this way,' Porridge said. 'You go that way.' He pointed.

I shook my head.

'No, you go that way,' I said.

'What's the difference?'

Thick, see?

'The tunnel,' I told him. 'I'm not allowed to go in there.' Porridge didn't know about the tunnel. 'Come on, I'll show you.'

Round the bend, past the trees, the mouth of the tunnel was dark and dripping with water. The canal and the towpath went right through it. It was miles long and dark all the way. Anything could be in there. Monsters, sea-snakes, creepy crawlies. An OCTOPUS.

'An octopus?' Porridge didn't believe me.

'With long tentacles that reach out of the water and drag you in,' I said, making slurping noises. 'Before it eats you.'

Porridge peered into the tunnel. A long, long way away, there was a little spot of light at the other end. In between there was only darkness and dripping water. He looked like he believed me now.

That's when we heard it.

'Yip, yip, yip.'

It came from inside the tunnel.

'That's Scruff,' I shouted. 'Come on.'

Porridge grabbed my jumper.

'What about the monsters, the sea-snake, the creepy-crawlies. The octopus?'

I grabbed his jumper.

'We have to get Scruff before they do, come on!'

We ran into the dark tunnel. The towpath was wet and slippery. Beside it, the canal looked very black. Water dripped into it from the roof. We stopped running and listened. It sounded like something slithery was swimming along beside us in the canal.

'We had better get out of here quick,' Porridge whispered.

'No! Listen.'

'Yip, yip, yip.' Scruff still sounded far away.

'We can't leave him here.' I dragged Porridge along the towpath. Crump! I fell over something lumpy and wet. The thing wriggled about under me. I squealed.

'Is it the octopus?' Porridge yelled.

'Yip, yip, yip,' the thing yelped. It was Scruff! I felt for him in the dark. My fingers touched something rough and wriggly and lumpy . . . it was a sack!

'Yip, yip!'

'Is that you, Scruff?'

The bundle wriggled even more. 'Yip!'

It was a sack, all right. Tied at the top. And Scruff was inside it. Porridge leaned over.

'Come on,' he hissed. 'Before the octopus gets us. You can untie it after we're out of the tunnel.'

I picked the sack up.

'It's all right, Scruff,' I said. 'I'll let you out soon.'

Then we turned round to head back to the entrance of the tunnel.

Porridge yelled.

In front of us was a huge, black, hunchbacked shape. It was the canal monster! Porridge dived behind me. I could feel him shaking. Inside the sack in my arms, Scruff was going crazy.

'Yip, yip, yip, yip!' he yelped.

'What are you doing with my sack?' a rough, deep voice demanded. The monster had a man's voice. 'Give me that.' And he grabbed for me.

Before I could do anything, Porridge jumped between us.

'Don't you touch my sister,' he shouted. Then he went for the man, punching and kicking. 'Run,' Porridge yelled.

I ran. Holding tight to the sack with Scruff inside it, I ran as hard as I could for the other end of the tunnel. Feet ran after me, getting nearer and nearer. I looked round. It was Porridge. And he had a hunchback now! He'd become a monster too! The big, black shape was running behind him. They were catching up with me. I ran, as hard as I could, for the daylight at the end of the tunnel. I wasn't going to make it before they caught me. Things couldn't get any worse, could they?

The end of the tunnel got bigger and bigger, brighter and brighter. I was nearly there. Nearly out. Then a great huge beast stepped between me and the daylight. Everything went dark again. The beast waved huge arms like tentacles. It was the octopus!

Splooge! I pelted right into the middle of it. It was soft and shuddery.

'Ooh! You've fair winded me,' it growled. It was Tina!

Splat! Porridge pelted into her too.

'Mum,' he yelled. 'That man's chasing us.'

'Oh, is he now,' Tina rumbled. Her voice growled and roared down the tunnel. I looked round at the man. He was so close now, I could see his eyes. They were big and white and starey. Tina pushed Porridge and me behind her.

THUMP! She socked the man with her huge sausage fist. The man fell back on to the towpath. He was all floppy and just lay there making a bubbling sound. Tina scooped the man up and swung him over her shoulder.

'I was looking for Scruff,' she said. 'Lucky for you two. Come on. Home.'

Out in the daylight, I could see Porridge didn't have a hunchback. He had a sack too, over his shoulder. When we got home I put my sack down and untied the string round the top. Scruff jumped out, yelping, grinning and licking my face.

'The man didn't have a hunchback,' Porridge said. 'He had this sack over his shoulder. When he dropped it to get me, I grabbed it and ran.' He untied the string. Two brown eyes looked out of the sack. It was a wee brown dog.

'That's Scooter,' I said. 'He belongs to my pal, Zarinda.'

Tina was sitting on the man. There wasn't much of him sticking out. Just the top of his head and his feet. I felt fine having a volcano as a step-mother. She picked up the phone and phoned the police.

'We'll get this dognapper where he belongs,' she said. 'Behind bars.'

When the police came, they took Scooter home. Then they took the man who'd tried to steal the dogs away in their van. After we'd washed off the muck from the tunnel, Porridge came into my room.

'You were really brave going into that tunnel,' he said.

'You were really brave going for that man,' I said. Don't touch my sister, he'd shouted at the dognapper. His sister. Me?

'Look,' he pointed to the label sticking up at the back of his neck, 'I've got my jumper on the right way round.'

Well, I was his sister, wasn't I? And sisters are helpful, aren't they?

'Yeah,' I said, 'but you've got it the wrong way out.'

'How do you know?' he asked.

'Cause the label goes on the inside, dopey!'

THUMP! He whacked me.

'Stop mucking about, you two,' my dad shouted up.

Us two. Me and my brother, Porridge.

THUMP! I whacked him right back.

ANGUS McANGUS AND THE PIRATE'S TREASURE

Margaret Ryan

Angus McAngus was far too polite to be a pirate. Whenever he boarded an enemy ship he always said, 'Would you mind awfully if I took your jewels?' Or, 'Please may I have your gold?'

The people on board just laughed at him and threw him into the sea. He never managed to pinch anything.

His parrot, Big Budgie, was fed up with fishing him out of the water.

'Ma grannie's a fiercer pirate than you, Angus,' he said. 'Gie it up and get another job.'

'Very well,' said Angus, and he became a fisherman instead.

He built a house, which Big Budgie named 'Dunrobbin', on the edge of Loch Stooshie, and went fishing every day. But he wasn't much good at that either. Usually he caught nothing more than a few tiddlers or a bad cold but, one day, his fishing net dragged up an old Irn-Bru bottle. Inside it was a yellowing piece of paper. Angus teased it out and unrolled it carefully.

'It's a map of Stooshie village,' he cried, 'showing Mighty Morag's treasure buried near a gate post in a grassy place. I wonder where that could be. It's not the Main Street, that's full of cobbles. It's not the harbour, that's full of water.'

Big Budgie sighed. 'Whit aboot the park, Angus?'

'Of course,' cried Angus. 'Why didn't I think of that. The park is full of grass. We'll go there right away and dig up the treasure.'

'We'll do no such thing,' said Big Budgie. 'We'll wait till it's dark. We'll wait till after we've had our tea.'

When they had finished eating, Angus looked out of the window. 'It's dark now,' he said. 'Let's go and dig up Mighty Morag's treasure.'

'Haud oan, Angus,' said Big Budgie. 'Mighty Morag's a really fierce pirate. She eats her mince and tatties raw. Are you sure you want to nick her treasure?'

'I don't want to steal anybody's treasure,' said Angus, 'but, if I had some money, I could ask Cinders to marry me, and we could live happily ever after and have lots of little Cinderses and Anguses.'

'Cinders? You mean yon daft wee lassie in the baker's that always burns the morning rolls? Ah didnae know you fancied her!'

Angus McAngus blushed. 'The rolls are just well fired,' he said. 'They're not really burnt. Anyway I like them like that.'

They waited a while longer then made their way to the park. A pale moon slid out from behind a cloud as Angus McAngus spread out the map.

'Look,' he said. 'Starting at the gate post, the treasure is ten paces to the left and five paces to the right.'

He paced out the steps and began to dig.

He dug and dug and dug.

'I'm getting blisters on my thumb with all this digging,' he said.

'An' Ah'm gettin' cobwebs on ma bum just watching you,' said Big Budgie. 'Dig faster, Angus.'

Angus dug faster. Then CHINK CHUNK, his spade hit something hard.

'It's the treasure chest,' cried Angus, and lifted it out.

The treasure chest was very heavy. Angus staggered about under its weight.

'Come on,' hissed Big Budgie. 'The dawn's coming up. Let's get out of here.'

But Angus was looking around him.

'Wait a minute,' he said. 'What are all these notices in the park?'

**NO RUNNING, SKIPPING OR JUMPING.
NO EATING, DRINKING
OR WALKING ON THE GRASS.
NO CATS, NO DOGS
AND DEFINITELY NO DUCKS!**

There was another notice too that said PARK FOR SALE.

'This is a strange kind of park,' said Angus.

'Come ON, Angus,' hissed Big Budgie. 'Back to Dunrobbin before we're spotted.'

Back home Angus tried to open the treasure chest with a kitchen knife. But that was no good. He tried a kitchen fork. But that was no good either. Big Budgie sighed and opened it with his skeleton key.

The chest was full of gold.

'Hooray, we're rich,' cried Big Budgie. 'No need to live on fish any more. We can have black-puddin' suppers, deep-fried Mars bars and Chinese carry-outs.'

But Angus McAngus was thoughtful. 'I've been thinking,' he said.

'Never a good idea,' muttered Big Budgie.

'I've been thinking,' went on Angus, 'about all the little Anguses and Cinderses and Kirstys and Donalds in Stooshie village. Where will they play if there's no park?'

Big Budgie scratched his head with his claw. 'Give us a clue.'

'Nowhere,' cried Angus McAngus. 'I think that's terrible. I think we should give them somewhere to play. I think we should buy the park.'

'I told you thinking was never a good idea,' sighed Big Budgie. 'Cheerio, black-puddin' supper. Ta-ta, take-away.'

'Come on,' grinned Angus. 'We'll buy the park straight away.'

They bought the park from Harris Tweed, the lawyer in Main Street.

Harris Tweed rubbed his hands.

'You've made a good buy there, Angus McAngus,' he said. 'And for a bit more money, I could help you build houses in the park.'

'No thank you,' said Angus McAngus.

'What about a car park?'

'No thank you,' said Angus McAngus.

'What are you going to do with the park, then?'

'Make it into a pirate fun park,' grinned Angus McAngus, and hurried away to take down all the NO notices.

'We'll put up YES notices instead,' he said to Big Budgie.

**YES, YOU CAN RUN AND JUMP AND SKIP.
YES, YOU CAN PLAY WITH DOGS AND
CATS ON THE GRASS.
YES, YOU CAN HAVE A PICNIC, AND PLEASE
DON'T FORGET TO FEED THE DUCKS.**

Before long Angus was the talk of Stooshie village and in the queue at the baker's in Main Street . . .

'What do you think,' said Mrs Mornington to Miss Kelvin. 'That Angus McAngus has just bought the village park. Harris Tweed told me he's going to turn it into a pirate fun park with swings and roundabouts and bouncy castles. Perhaps even ducks. We can't have that. Imagine having a noisy fun park with messy ducks in the middle of Stooshie village. The very idea!'

'Don't worry, We'll put a stop to it,' said Miss Kelvin. 'And I think I know how.'

She had just started to whisper to her companion Mrs Mornington when Cinders, the baker's assistant, said, 'What can I get you, Miss Kelvin?'

'Knitting needles,' said Miss Kelvin.

'I'm sorry, we don't sell knitting needles,' said Cinders. 'You'll need to go along to Mrs Munro's wool shop for knitting needles.'

'What are you talking about?' snapped Miss Kelvin. 'I'll have my usual two buttered rolls, and no burnt ones like yesterday.'

'Stupid girl,' muttered Mrs Mornington as Cinders hurried away.

Meanwhile Angus had been busy. He spent a lot of the treasure money on bouncy castles and trampolines, and made a duckpond out of the hole where the treasure chest had been.

'This is much better fun than pirating,' he said to Big Budgie. 'I'll just go and pin up the posters now for the Grand Opening.'

The posters said:

**GRAND OPENING OF PIRATE
FUN PARK
NEXT SATURDAY AT 2 P.M.
COME DRESSED AS A PIRATE
FREE FOOD AND FUN.**

Big Budgie grinned. 'Ah've never seen you look so chirpy, Angus. But, gie me the posters. I'll fly round with them. It'll be quicker.'

Big Budgie flew all round the village with

the posters, but he was so busy thinking about the Grand Opening, he didn't notice two sneaky figures following him.

Angus could hardly wait for the Grand Opening day to arrive. To keep himself busy he went fishing, but he only caught an old pram. To keep himself busy he tidied up Dunrobbin, but Big Budgie didn't like being dusted. To keep himself busy he went to the baker's three times a day and bought all of Cinders's burnt – sorry – well-fired rolls.

'I've got something to ask you, Cinders,' he said finally.

'Yes?' breathed Cinders.

'Will you . . . ?'

'Yes?' breathed Cinders.

'Will you . . . ?'

'Yes?' breathed Cinders.

'Will you ma . . . make me more of these rolls?'

'OK,' sighed Cinders.

The day of the Grand Opening arrived and Angus and Big Budgie, dressed in their very best pirate uniforms, set out for the park. They fixed a Jolly Roger to the ribbon tied across the gate in a neat bow, and asked Cinders to come and officially open the park at two o'clock.

Cinders came, but nobody else did.

Angus and Big Budgie looked up and down the road. It was empty.

Then a really fierce pirate stomped up. She had I HATE PORRIDGE tattooed on her forehead and a real moustache.

'Mighty Morag,' gulped Angus. 'What are you doing here?'

'I've come to collect my treasure,' she said. 'My map rolled overboard on a wild and windy night, but I ken fine where I buried the treasure. It's yonder beneath that . . . *duck pond*? What's a duck pond doing where my treasure should be? Tell me right now, Angus McAngus, or I'll skelp your lugs till your head spins!'

'Erm well, it's like this, Mighty Morag,' gulped Angus, crossing his fingers behind his back, 'I found your treasure map, but I thought you must have fallen overboard too, so I decided to use the treasure to make a fun park in your honour. We're going to call it the Mighty Morag Fun Park.'

Mighty Morag wrinkled her brow and stroked her moustache. 'A pirate fun park in my honour, you say?'

Angus, Big Budgie and Cinders swallowed hard and nodded.

Mighty Morag thought for a moment, then a strange thing happened. A large tear rolled down her cheek, followed by another and another.

'I ran away to sea when I was wee because all the swings in this park were tied up and there was no fun anywhere,' she sniffed.

'Well, there'll be plenty of fun now,' said Angus.

'When?' asked Mighty Morag. 'I'm here, but nobody else is. Why aren't folks here enjoying my fun park. Go and find out right now.'

'Ah'm away already,' said Big Budgie. 'Back in two ticks.'

TICK TICK.

Big Budgie flew back with some posters in his beak.

'Here's why nobody came. I found out that Mrs Mornington and Miss Kelvin had sneaked round after me and changed the posters. Look . . .' GRAND OPENING CANCELLED.

'CANCELLED!' roared Mighty Morag. 'These miserable wee scunners have dared to cancel MY Grand Opening!'

'Don't worry, Mighty Morag,' soothed Angus. 'We'll go round and tell everyone about the Grand Opening ourselves. You stay here and keep an eye open for the wee scunners . . . I mean, those wretched ladies.'

The friends told everyone they met about the Grand Opening and before long people dressed as pirates flocked to the fun park.

'A pirate fun park,' yelled the children. 'Brilliant!'

'Race you to the bouncy castles,' cried the mums and dads.

'Wait for us,' said the grans and grandads.

'This is more like it,' grinned Angus, handing out the free ice creams.

He was just taking Cinders to feed the ducks when he spied two strange looking pirates. They wore pink eye patches, frilly pink wigs and carried shopping bags from Jenners Department Store.

'That looks like Mrs Mornington and Miss Kelvin,' whispered Cinders to Angus.

'But they didn't want the fun park so why are they here?'

'We'll follow them and find out,' said Angus.

They spotted Big Budgie and Mighty Morag by the trampolines, and the four of them secretly followed Mrs Mornington and Miss Kelvin round the park. The frilly pink pirates made their way to the bouncy castles. When they thought no one was looking, they went into their bags and took out their knitting needles. Then they raised them up ready to puncture the bouncy castles.

Mighty Morag pounced.

'Gotcha, you pair of miserable wee scunners!' she cried.

'We weren't doing anything,' cried Mrs Mornington and Miss Kelvin, and tried to hide the knitting needles behind their backs.

'And I'm no doin' anything either,' grinned Mighty Morag as she bounced them up and down on the bouncy castle till their teeth rattled and their legs turned to wobbly jelly.

Then Big Budgie dropped an ice cream on their heads.

'Have an ice day,' he cried as they wobbled away.

The people of Stooshie village loved the

fun park and when the Grand Opening day was over, they carried Angus and Cinders shoulder-high back to Dunrobbin. Big Budgie flew by himself, and nobody could lift Mighty Morag.

'That was a good idea you had to buy the park, Angus,' she said when they were back indoors and Big Budgie and Cinders had gone to make tea and toast. 'Why don't you stay on as park manager? I'll pay you well, and you can settle down and never go to sea again.'

'I'd like that,' grinned Angus.

Then Cinders and Big Budgie brought in the tea things and Angus had another good idea. He went down on one knee in front of Cinders and said, 'Cinders, will you marry me?'

'Yes, yes, yes,' cried Cinders. 'I thought you'd never ask.' And she threw her arms round his neck and kissed him.

Mighty Morag grinned and cooled her tea with her pirate's hat. 'Don't you just love a happy ending, Big Budgie?' she said.

'Oh aye,' sighed Big Budgie. 'An' ah'll probably get to love burnt toast as well.'

THE REAL WORLD

Catherine MacPhail

'Joseph Connor! Are you listening to me? This is very important. Don't you want to save the Amazonian rainforests?' Miss Gower shouted across the classroom at the top of her voice.

Joe looked up slowly, then went back to biting his nails. 'Not particularly, Miss,' he said.

Daft old bat, he thought. The Amazonian rainforest? He'd never heard of anything more boring in his life. Miss Gower was always going on about saving something. Last week it had been tigers in India. The week before that it had been whales. Thank goodness, Joe thought, there was only one Miss Gower. Definitely an endangered species. And once she was gone, that would be the end of her. And it couldn't come too soon in Joe's opinion.

She was still staring at him and shaking her head. 'You will amount to nothing, Joseph Connor, unless you start taking an interest in your planet.'

He'll amount to nothing. Ha! That was a good one, considering she was only a teacher ... and from England. You just can't amount to less than that.

*

He said this to his pal, Solid, when they were going out through the school gates. Solid got his nickname because he was built like a brick shed. A hurricane couldn't topple him. He was a good guy to be pals with. Especially if you were the size of Joe, who was just about the smallest boy in the class.

'I mean, my dad says that Miss Gower just doesn't live in the real world. If she lived where we live, boarded-up houses, unemployment. I mean, war-torn Bosnia's got nothing on our estate. She'd know all about the real world then, eh? That's what my dad says.'

'She's always picking on you, Joe,' Solid told him, as if he didn't already know that. Big guy, but not much in the brain department. 'How is that, do you think?'

'Because, Solid, I am not the least bit interested in her Amazonian rainforests, her tigers and her whales.'

'What is an Amazonian rainforest by the way, Joe?' he asked.

Solid assumed that Joe knew everything, and Joe refused to admit that he didn't. Joe explained. 'It's up in the Amazon, naturally, and it's like a big wood and . . . eh . . . they get an awful lot of rain. I mean, as if we don't get enough bad weather here in Scotland, and nobody tries to save us.'

He left Solid at the bus stop and wandered homeward. Miss Gower was always trying to get him to listen and learn. But what was the point? As his dad said, he probably would end up on the dole, like everyone else on the estate. Like his dad. The thought kind of depressed him but he tried not to think about it. He planned to forget Miss Gower and school, at least until tomorrow.

It was then he noticed she was walking in front of him, and she was talking to herself.

Daft old bat, he thought again, and this woman's supposed to be in charge of my education. No wonder I'm thick.

He followed at a discreet distance. He knew at the next corner that he would be going one way, and Miss Gower would be going the other. She even looked dotty. As she was talking to herself she was rummaging in her massive leather bag. She carried a big golf umbrella hooked on her arm. It was almost as big as she was. She had springy grey hair that looked like a scouring pad had been stuck on her head and a permanently twitching nose as if she was always smelling something funny, or was just about to sneeze.

Suddenly, she did sneeze and half the contents of her bag exploded on to the pavement. She darted her eyes all around, almost as if she was scared, as if she expected to see something. Joe jumped into a doorway. He didn't want her to see *him*. She was on her knees, scooping up her purse and her glasses and her handkerchief and stuffing them all back into her bag. Then she clutched it to her, had another furtive look around and began scurrying off down the street.

Nutty as a fruitcake, Joe decided. If only the headmaster could see her now, he wouldn't keep telling them what a wonderful lady Miss Gower is. He would have her in a straitjacket before you could say Amazonian rainforest.

Joe was about to go his own way when something glinting on the pavement caught his eye. He moved closer, intrigued in spite of himself.

Her keys. The daft old bat had dropped her keys. He bent and picked them up. Well, he wasn't going after her with them. He had better things to do. He had a burger and a Coke waiting for him at home. He looked at the keys in his hand. She would probably be locked out if he didn't go after her.

Tough. Not his problem. Why should he

go after her? She could be locked out for one night. Ha! She'd know what the real world felt like then.

Mind you, it did look as if it was going to rain. He threw the keys up and caught them. Joe, Joe, Joe, he thought, why are you such a nice guy?

And he went off after his teacher.

He caught sight of her as she disappeared into an alley. He followed. Just before he turned after her, he heard a scuffle and the sound of Miss Gower sneezing several times. He peeked around the corner. Two really big men were struggling with her. Joe began to shout. He began to run.

'Hey! Hey, you two. Leave her be!'

The men turned, and Joe got the fright of his life. They didn't look human. They were wearing the scariest-looking masks that Joe had ever seen. They had to be. They stepped away from Miss Gower, who was lying in a heap by this time, and they began to run at Joe.

Suddenly, Miss Gower, daft Miss Gower, took a swipe at their ankles with her umbrella and brought them down. Joe could hardly believe it. He almost cheered. It was a brilliant move. He ran and stopped right in front of them. Their masks looked eerie in

the darkened alley. Suddenly, Joe let out one almighty sneeze and covered them with the contents of his nose. They covered their faces and began to yell as if they'd been sprayed with acid. Then they got to their feet and in a flash they were off down the alley.

'And don't come back or I'll sneeze on ye again!' Joe shouted after them. He turned to Miss Gower. She was watching him with her mouth hanging open. If she looked daft before, she looked really stupid now.

'You're the One,' she said, in amazement.

'Eh?' Joe asked, helping her to her feet.

'You frightened them off. You sneezed.'

She gasped and clutched at her throat. 'You, Joseph . . . are the one I was sent here to find.'

Nutty as a fruitcake, Joe thought again. 'The one . . . what?' he asked her.

She looked all around as if she was expecting someone to hear her. 'The new . . .' she took a deep breath. 'Keeper.'

Joe took a deep breath of his own before he repeated, 'The Keeper?'

'The Keeper of Good. You saw their faces, Joseph. They were demons.'

'They were wearing masks,' he told her.

She shook her head and her scouring pad wiggled. 'They were horrible to behold,' she said.

'Och, I've got neighbours uglier than that.'

But she wouldn't listen.

'I was sent here for a purpose, Joseph. To find the New Keeper. Just like you, I was chosen to defend all that is right. To keep the demons from invading our world. Now, as I grow old, I must pass the ring on to someone else.' She took from her finger the heavy silver ring she always wore and handed it to Joe.

'I can't take that, Miss,' he said.

But she insisted, slipping it on his finger herself.

'It doesn't fit, Miss,' he said.

'It will, Joe. It will.'

Joe suddenly felt sorry for the poor old soul. The attack must have pushed her over the edge. He decided to play along with her. 'So, how will I know these demons? Do they all look like that?'

'Whenever they are close by, Joseph, you will sneeze. The germs you let loose from your body are so potent, so full of pure goodness, they cannot fight it.'

Well, it was handy to know the next time he flicked a bogey he was spreading pure goodness all around. Wait till he told his mother. She'd never get him into trouble for picking his nose again.

'So you've been fighting these demons for a while, then?'

'Since I was your age. I was chosen as the Keeper. But now my sneezes do not have the power they once had.'

Joe tried not to giggle at that bit. Whoever heard of a superhero whose special power was a sneeze? At least he should be able to leap tall buildings in a single bound. Or have X-ray vision. But a sneeze.

Miss Gower was rattling on. 'The demons come into our world to cause wars, to create chaos, to destroy. They tried to cause the Great Nuclear War.'

'There wasn't a Great Nuclear War, Miss.'

He wasn't very good at history, but he knew that.

She nodded. 'Thanks to me there wasn't, Joseph.' She placed a hand on his shoulder. 'It is our destiny to protect mankind. In the next few years you will discover powers you never knew you had. You will be the one who saves the world.'

Nutty as a fruitcake, Joe kept thinking as he wandered home.

Next morning in class, Joe stuck his chewing gum under his desk and leaned back in his seat. Miss Gower was rummaging through her bag again. All at once, to his complete embarrassment, she looked up at him and winked.

Joe glanced around quickly to make sure no one had seen. He had thought perhaps he had dreamed up the men attacking his teacher, dreamed up her crazy story, but here she was winking at him as if they both knew something no one else knew. And he still had her ring on his finger; and funny thing, this morning it actually fitted. His fingers must have swollen during the night.

What a crazy story she had told him. Demons trying to invade the world. And him, Joe Connor, the Keeper? Saviour of the world? Rubbish.

Joe sat quietly for a while, thinking. It *would* be exciting to be a superhero.

If only it could be true. It sounded so much better than the real world his dad had always told him to expect. And you never know, it might be true. Stranger things have happened. Not much stranger, however.

What was the Boy Scouts' motto? Be Prepared.

Maybe, he decided, he'd better be prepared. Just in case.

Suddenly, to the surprise of his classmates, he called out to his teacher. 'Hey, Miss Gower? Tell us again about that Amazonian rainforest.' He studied his nails. 'Who knows . . . I might be the very boy to save it.'

THE RAFT RACE

Alison Prince

Last summer, we reckoned we'd win the raft race. Our family's team was a really good one – we're great swimmers and handy at things like raft-building. We run a farm down the south end of the island, so we're used to tying stuff up with baler twine and using odds and ends. Small farms are like that.

I was in the team, of course. I'm only nine, but I'm the two-lengths champion of Cuddy Brae Primary. And you need someone small, because the rules say one from each team has to ride on the raft while the other three swim it out to the marker buoy. The first team to get there wins. And you've to build your raft first. So we had Dad and me and Auntie May, who's quite fat but floats like a cork, and my cousin Helen. She's Auntie May's daughter, and she runs the ladies' football team. They beat the Young Farmers three-one last week. Like I say, we thought we were in with a good chance.

All the other teams were saying the same thing, even no-hopers like the lot from the Glen Beag bar. The McEwans fancied themselves because Robbie's in the lifeboat crew but, as Dad pointed out, you don't get to do much swimming in those great boots and yellow oilskins. Robbie was good, though, we had to admit that. The last lot of winners were the Adamsons, because Mrs Adamson used to be a PE teacher. This year, she was in the finals of the all-island bowls championship, on the same afternoon as the raft race, which was lucky for us. Jenny from the post office was taking her place, but she's better at badminton. Doesn't like rough water.

Davey Morrison and some of his mates from the fish farm were talked about as a good team, and four people from the Tourist Board had entered, though everyone said that lot couldn't sail a plastic duck in a bath. And there were the Suttons.

Nobody was sure about the Suttons. They only had a holiday house here, and we didn't think that should count. But Mum heard Mr Sutton saying in the paper shop that the local teams were scared of being made to look silly, so we couldn't bar them after that. They just had to be honourably beaten.

It's not that we're unfriendly. Most of our visitors are fine. Some of them have been coming for years and they're like members of the family, but the ones who own houses here can be a bit much, specially the sort who only come for a couple of weeks in the summer. They arrive with all this stuff they've brought with them from a mainland supermarket, and never come into our shops except for milk and the *Radio Times*.

The Suttons were like that. And they complained about the bottle banks because they didn't like looking at them, and kicked up a fuss about the travelling fair. It was only a bouncy castle and a wee roundabout, but they said they came to the island for peace and quiet. They kept moaning on about the music and the kids tooting their wee car horns, and in the end the guy packed up and went somewhere else. He's never been back.

There were four Suttons, a mum and dad who played golf and two girls. The older one was almost grown up, and this year she'd brought her boyfriend with her. The younger one was about ten, and dead keen on horses, so she spent most of her time at the trekking centre. Dad said he couldn't understand why girls never felt like that about cows.

The morning of the race was chilly. It wasn't actually raining, but the sky was grey, and a stiff wind ruffled the sea.

Mum said, 'Good thing we've plenty of

stuff for the bonfire, you'll be frozen when you come out.' She hates swimming. She says she feels about it like the sheep do about sheep-dip.

'We'll be fine,' Dad said. 'Swimming gets you warm. And, anyway, we're going to win four nice, dry T-shirts, aren't we?'

'Huh,' said Mum. 'You'll be lucky.'

'You just wait,' said Dad.

I hoped he was right. The T-shirts had been on display in the paper shop for nearly three weeks. They were bright yellow, with WORLD CHAMPION printed across them, and in smaller letters, CUDDY BRAE RAFT RACE. Stella Murchie who makes curtains has this machine that can print anything. Before she got it, the raft-race prize was just a bottle of whisky, but I think the T-shirts are better.

The race wasn't due to start until two-thirty, but we all went along earlier to help Mum and the support team get the fire started. Jim Barr was there with his van backed on to the edge of the grass and cable all over the place, fixing up the public address system. Down on the stones there were seven piles of raft-making materials, one for each team. They were all the same – four empty oil drums, eight planks and some cross-pieces, and a lot of rope. Each one had a stake beside it, driven into the sand, holding a bit of cardboard with a number on it. Ian from the Co-op was patrolling up and down with his sheepdogs, just in case anyone thought they'd start tying a few knots before the whistle blew.

'I brought rugs,' Mum said, glancing at the sea severely. 'And blankets. They're in the boot.'

'Ah, come on,' said Dad. 'We're not talking Scott of the Antarctic here, it's just a wee dip. Once we're in, it'll be great.'

'Speak for yourself,' said Helen, turning up the collar of her fleece jacket. 'I must be mad.'

The ambulance arrived, and Auntie May said, 'They only come for the free hot dogs.' Then the minister got out of her car with her two spaniels, who rushed into the sea then shook themselves all over the ladies from the Women's Rural who were trying to get the barbecue started. The minister said, 'Sorry,' and Dickie Sprat waved his half-bottle of whisky at the dogs and said, 'Down, ye brutes.' Nobody took any notice. He was only there to cheer on the team from the Glen Beag bar.

Alan Ritchie came put-putting over from the pier in one of his hire-boats with a flag that said JUDGE flying from the mast, and

Jim's amplified voice rang out, 'Ladies and gentlemen, here comes our referee for this afternoon – Alan Ritchie!' Everyone clapped. Alan's dead good at judging the dog show.

Then a big Volvo bumped across the grass and parked by the ambulance, and four spacemen got out. At least, that's what it looked like. They were in black rubber zipped up to their chins, and they were putting on large flippers. It was the Suttons.

'Good grief,' Dad said. 'They've got wetsuits.'

'That's not fair,' said Auntie May.

The spacemen were coming towards us down the bank of stones, lifting their knees high because of the flippers, and one of them said, 'Nothing unfair about it. You could have wetsuits if you wanted.' We could see he was the boyfriend. The older girl was holding his hand, wearing a summer dress and clearly not a team member. The other three were the Sutton mum and dad and the horse-mad girl, who looked as if she wasn't enjoying it much.

Muttered discussions were going on. Somebody asked the minister what she thought about wetsuits and flippers, but she chickened out and said it was a matter for the referee.

'WHAT ABOUT WETSUITS AND FLIPPERS?' Jim asked through his mike.

Alan bawled back from the boat, 'We don't have a rule about wetsuits. Never needed one. But NO FLIPPERS!'

Grumbling, the four spacemen sat down and took their flippers off. Nobody watched – or at least, we pretended not to. Mrs Abernethy from the Rural started putting beefburgers on the barbecue, and there were clouds of smoke and a sizzling sound.

'STARTER'S ORDERS,' Jim said. 'TEAM LEADERS COME AND DRAW YOUR LOTS FOR PLACES, PLEASE.'

This was to decide which pile of raft-making stuff each of us got. We were drawn next to the furthest along, between the McEwans and the Morrisons. When everyone was in the right place, Jim said, 'ARE YOU READY?' And blew the whistle.

We all leaped into action. Our team knew exactly what to do, being old hands at it. The first thing was to get a couple of loops of rope round each oil drum, using the free ends to lash them to a spar in pairs. We got that done, then joined the spars with cross-pieces – but we'd learned last year that the whole thing can go off-square once it's afloat, and then you're in trouble. So we put diagonals across this time, and tied them firmly with a couple of planks on top.

It took quite a long time, and some of the teams were in the water before we'd finished. The McEwans had gone for speed, and so had the spacemen, who were out there quicker than any of us. I looked back as we hauled the raft into the water, and saw the Glen Beag bar team laughing and falling about, and the Tourist Board seemed to be arguing among themselves.

I clambered on to our raft and shouted, 'Straight ahead!' It was the rider's job to do the navigating, because the swimmers were behind the raft and couldn't see anything. I couldn't see much myself, because the raft was pitching about in the choppy sea, and waves kept breaking over me. The McEwans's raft was tilting sideways, and Alec, their rider, was nearly off it. I caught a glimpse of the Adamsons, but they were badly off course. Jenny was their rider, but she had her eyes shut, and shrieked every time she got doused with water. I couldn't look back – I was too busy hanging on – but I could see the spacemen ahead of us. The horse-mad girl was lying flat on the raft, not doing any navigation at all, and they had swimmers on either side. Their raft wasn't much good – a couple of spars had come off it, and a drum was breaking loose – but at least when you're in the front, nobody's going to crash into you. Judging by the yells and laughter behind me, that was happening a lot.

'Left a bit!' I shouted. 'Come on, come on!' But it was no good. The spacemen were almost at the marker buoy. Unless their raft completely fell apart, they were going to win.

And they did. I saw Alan's flag go up in the boat. It was hard to hear what Jim was saying through the PA, but people were clapping politely. There was more of a cheer when we got to the buoy a minute or two later. Dad and Helen and Auntie May leaned

their arms on the raft, panting, and Dad said, 'Well done, folks. At least the raft held together.'

A spar went bucking by from the spacemen's disintegrating raft, and there seemed to be a lot of frantic swimming going on. Then I heard a scream.

Alan Ritchie's engine roared as he gunned the boat towards the floating wreckage, and a woman shrieked, 'She's gone!'

Dad struck out towards her, swimming fast, and Helen followed.

'I can see her!' Alan yelled from the boat. 'There, look!'

I didn't know where he meant. I've never been scared of the sea, but suddenly the depth below me was frightening, and I clung tighter to the raft. Then Dad came up, quite near us, and he had his arm round the girl. Her dark hair was all over his shoulder. Other swimmers were round him, but it was hard to get the girl on to the raft, she was so limp and heavy.

'Mind out,' Robbie McEwan said to me. I slipped into the water and he hauled himself on to the raft – and Dad got on too. They turned the girl over and Robbie started to press steadily on her back. Water was coming out of her mouth. Then she coughed and retched as if she was being sick. 'Good lass,' Robbie said, still working on her. 'Come on, now.'

The other Suttons were round the raft, hanging on to it. Mrs Sutton was crying, and her husband was holding her. More boats were coming, one of them with the ambulance crew. They lifted the girl into the boat and wrapped her up. One of the men looked at me and said, 'You all right, son?'

I said I was, though I felt a bit shaky. We paddled the raft to the shore with lots of people helping, and Mum wrapped me in a big towel and rubbed me as if I was a little kid again.

The girl was OK. Apparently she got hit on the head by a spar when their raft broke up. She said she didn't remember much else, she only came to in the boat. She's really nice – her name's Tiggy. We got to know each other after they came round to say a big thank you. I went pony-trekking with her once or twice, and it was great. I hadn't tried it before. Her family never wore their Raft Race Champion T-shirts round the village, though. Maybe they did back in London. I'll ask Tiggy next year.

JACK'S
AUNTIE'S MAGIC!

Ann McDonagh Bengtsson

'She's weird and she hates boys! Please, Mum,' Jack pleaded, 'not Auntie Sheena! I'll do anything, but don't send me to her.'

'Somebody has to look after you while I'm on this course in Edinburgh, Jack,' his mum said. 'There's nobody else. You have to go to Skye. That's it!'

'Can't I stay with Graeme?'

'Graeme's family are away.'

'I'll be OK on my own!'

'You're ten years old, Jack. It's against the law,' Mum insisted.

'But, Mum, the last time Auntie Sheena came to Glasgow, she threw out all the sausages and pies in the fridge and insisted on everyone eating veggies and organic rubbish.'

'So she likes health food. It's good for you, Jack,' Mum said firmly.

'And she made me wear that horrible jumper she knitted, to school. I looked like a sheep. All the kids went "baaah". I'd to thump a few of them to get some respect. Was I glad when she finally cleared off. She's weird!'

'Oh, it's only a week. Stop whining. Now come on, we've got to get you to the bus, the driver says he'll keep an eye on you.'

'But, Mum.'

'Give Sheena a chance, Jack, you'll see, she's magic!'

'Magic? She is not! Oh, do I need that, Mum?' Jack felt stupid as she tied a label on his rucksack. *Jack Baxter, c/o Sheena MacDonald, Storr Cottage, Near Portree, Isle of Skye.* Embarrassing, he thought, I'm just like a parcel. All that's missing is the stamp.

The journey took for ever, all the way up the Highlands across the bridge to Skye, then up the long, winding road by the sea to Portree.

'This is you, laddie!' the driver said, stopping the bus in the middle of nowhere. It was so misty, Jack could hardly see a thing.

He climbed down and stood there as the bus disappeared into the mist. 'What a dump,' he shivered.

Sheena suddenly appeared from behind a rock, dressed in a long cloak. 'So, you're here,' she said in a hissy voice. She looked much taller and thinner than Jack remembered from the year before.

'Looks like it,' Jack replied.

'Right, what are you waiting for?' She led the way across the road, heading right through a field.

'Oi! Hang on!' Jack hared after her, tripping on the lumps of heather and dodging big clumps of bracken. A chilly wind rose from the sea and blew the mist about; spots of rain began to fall. 'This isn't funny!' he muttered under his breath. 'I'll never last a week.'

'Watch your feet,' Sheena warned, but it was too late.

'Oh, yuk!' Jack stepped into a pile of soggy sheep droppings.

'Never mind,' she called over her shoulder. 'It'll wash off when we cross the burn.'

'What do you mean?' Jack panted.

'You'll see.' Before they had gone much further, they were faced with a narrow stream dotted with stepping stones, some of them half under water.

'Don't fall in, for goodness' sake!' Sheena said.

'What? Where's she gone?' Jack blinked. One minute she was on the misty bank, the next she was on the other side. 'How did you do that?' he gasped.

'Easy, I flew!' She grinned, showing pointed teeth. 'Come on then.'

'Flew?' Jack looked at the fast-flowing water. 'You jumped,' he said.

169

'Then you do it.'

'Nah!' Carefully he edged across on the stones, almost falling in twice and getting icy water in his trainers.

'Not bad,' Sheena laughed. 'I was sure you'd be dripping like a bat in the rain!'

'Dripping like a bat?' Jack shook his head. Sheena was strange.

'Oh,' she said, 'here's Angus.'

A big hairy man came out of the white, drifting mist. Everything about Angus was hairy. His head, his face, his jumper, trousers and socks. Only his shoes weren't, but they were covered in muck and looked a bit hairy too. They began talking in a strange language, looking at his wet feet and laughing as if he wasn't there.

'Did you lose this?' Angus took a coin out of thin air and handed it to Jack. 'Or is this yours?'

'What?' Jack gawped as he pulled another one from his beard.

'No? Then I'll keep them.' Angus gave a hairy grin and disappeared as silently as he had come.

'Where did he go?'

'Home. You'll see him tomorrow,' she said. 'Here we are.' The cottage appeared through the mist, tucked in a hollow by the seashore. It looked normal enough from the outside, but when they went into the kitchen Jack's eyes nearly popped out of his head.

A huge black cat sat by a big black cooker where pots of strange smelling stuff bubbled and hissed. An enormous kettle spurted out steam in clouds as it boiled. The smell of whatever she was burning tickled his nose. Herbs and grasses of all sorts hung in bunches from beams across the kitchen. An old-fashioned broom stood in the corner.

'So what are you gawking at?' she asked. 'Never seen a proper kitchen before? None of your fridges and microwaves here!'

'Yes . . . no . . . nothing . . . it's OK.'

'Leave your stinky trainers in the hall,' she

said. 'Here.' She gave him a pair of socks as hairy as Angus's face.

Jack was glad Graeme and the others couldn't see how daft he looked once he'd put them on.

'Now what's this junk?' She went head first into his bag, her long nose twitching in disgust. 'Well for a start you won't need these.' She emptied his packet of favourite breakfast bars straight into a box. 'Nor these!' They were followed by his sweeties and crisps.

'Oh, come on,' Jack protested. 'I'll starve.'

'You'll do no such thing,' she replied. 'Sit there.' She pointed at the table.

As he sat down, the cat got up, arched its back and spat, looking at him evilly with green eyes.

'Pandor doesn't like wee boys, or big ones either,' Sheena gave a pointy toothed grin.

'Great!' Jack slipped into the seat, keeping a careful eye on the cat as it lay down again and curled up in front of the cooker.

Sheena cut some thick slices of stuff that looked a bit like bread. 'This is bannock,' she said. 'You can spread it with butter and jam.'

'But I don't like this kind of food,' he protested. 'Can't I have some oven chips?'

'Forget it!' she snapped.

Jack forced down a few mouthfuls. It tasted OK with lots of jam, but he wasn't going to admit that.

All evening he hung about feeling home-sick. Outside the wind rose and howled round the cottage. When he finally climbed into bed in a room with a low ceiling and only a candle for a light, he wished he was safely back home with his computer games and posters. Tossing and turning, he planned his escape. 'I'll find my way back to Glasgow if it kills me,' he muttered.

The wind moaned back at him. 'Oh no, you won't,' it said.

'Oh yes, I will,' he answered out loud, but inside he felt a bit scared.

'I'm off to Portree,' Sheena said next morning. 'There's bannock if you get hungry, and some fruit. You'll not be on your own. Pandor will look after you.' She nodded over to where it lay.

'A cat can't look after me,' Jack replied scornfully.

Pandor got up and glared at him, hissing and spitting loudly.

'All right, pal, no offence!' Jack said hastily. 'But can't I just come with you?' Portree was on the way to Glasgow, even if it was still on Skye. Maybe he could give her the slip.

'No,' she said. 'Anyway, Angus will be coming by. He'll take you fishing.'

'If he wants.' Jack had been fishing once in the River Clyde, but he hadn't caught a thing.

'Then I'm off,' she said.

He heard the door close.

'Time to leg it!' he muttered.

Pandor lay between him and the door. Every time he tried to get past, it arched its back and spat. 'You stupid cat!' Jack said angrily, but he wasn't going to chance it attacking him. 'I suppose I'd better eat some of this disgusting rubbish and wait till the cat clears off.'

He had wolfed down a couple of slices of bannock with jam, when the door opened and Hairy Angus came in. 'So it's you that's coming with me, then?' he asked in the same soft hissy voice as Sheena.

'Er . . . yes,' Jack agreed. Even going out in a boat was better than being left alone with Sheena's cat. Escape could wait.

Hairy Angus bent down and took a ten-pence piece from Pandor's ear, handing it to Jack. The cat didn't even blink, let alone spit.

'How do you do that?' Jack said, scuttling after him as he headed down to the waterside.

'Just magic! Here, you better put this on.'

Hairy Angus handed him a life jacket.

Jack was about to protest when he saw the huge waves in the bay. 'OK,' he said.

'This is what we use,' Angus held up a line with silvery hooks all along the lower part. 'When we hit a shoal of mackerel, they'll be coming in two at a time.'

Yeah, in your dreams, Jack thought.

'Here they are!' Angus yelled after they'd rowed far out into the bay. He began to cast the line.

'Wow,' Jack gasped.

Angus hauled in fish by the hooks-full. 'Get moving, boy!' he shouted, and even with Jack's help they could hardly keep up, they caught so many.

'What the heck is happening?' Jack called above the noise of the ocean.

'Och, just a wee bit more magic.' Angus looked at him sideways.

Jack noticed his eyes glittered strangely. What's up with the guys around here? he wondered uneasily.

Angus didn't let him out of his sight all day, but nearly drove him mad, pulling coins out of his mouth and hair and grinning all the time. He was still at the cottage that evening when Sheena came back and hung her cloak in the hallway. Escape was out of the question for now.

'You two cook that mackerel,' she said. 'I'll get the rest of dinner.'

'You can't cook with that!' Jack said as hairy Angus went outside and put lumps of brown, fibrous, earthy stuff into a pile and began to light it.

'Oh no?' Angus grinned and watched Jack's face change as the brown earth glowed. He grilled the skewered fish slowly over it. Spurts of fat ran on to the fire, spluttering and sparking. 'Here, try one.' Hairy Angus handed him a crispy mackerel on a plate.

'I haven't got a fork,' Jack said.

'Use your fingers, laddie!' Angus glared at him. 'Fish is good for the brains. You need to eat a lot of fisssh,' he hissed.

'OK,' Jack said quickly, not liking the nasty look in hairy Angus's eyes. 'Oh, it's not bad,' he added in surprise once he had tasted it.

'Come in with the fish, soup's ready,' Sheena called.

They put the rest on a tin plate and wandered back inside. Sheena was standing over the big pot on the cooker, singing a strange chant as she threw herbs and things into it, stirring all the time.

Pandor rubbed against her legs. Sheena looks just like a witch, Jack thought idly, then froze. His eyes slid to the broomstick in the corner. It was all he could do not to gasp in horror. It began to make sense. Wait a minute . . . was that what Mum meant when she said that Sheena was magic? Was he stuck with a witch? No wonder he thought she was weird. Hissy voice, big teeth, the strange smelling cooking pot, odd language, black cat, broomstick . . . it was all there when you put it together. Bet she could turn me to stone if she wanted, he thought with a shiver.

'Sorry,' he croaked. 'I'm not very hungry . . . in fact, I'm quite tired. Er . . . goodnight. I've some games mags to read.'

'Please yourself. More for us.' Sheena shrugged and handed Angus a plate of green soup.

'Just the very thing to put hair on your teeth!' Angus said, with a hairy grin.

Oh no! Jack thought he could live without hairy teeth, so he fled.

That night he hardly slept a wink as eerie night noises rose and fell outside. Next morning he crept out of bed, collected his things and slowly edged towards the door. Just as he got outside and started towards the road, Sheena came round the corner, clutching her broomstick. 'Got you!' she said showing a load of pointy teeth.

'Owya!' Jack yelped and started to run, followed by Sheena, the cat and Hairy Angus who, as usual, appeared from nowhere.

Breath rasping in his throat, Jack made it across the field. He began to race towards where the bus had dropped him, when he tripped on a stone and fell flat on his face.

They were on him right away. Angus hauled him to his feet. 'What on earth are you trying to do, you daft laddie?' he asked angrily, shaking Jack till his teeth rattled.

'Running away!' Jack shouted. 'She's a witch, with her funny songs, cloak, pot and broomstick, and you're not much better, telling me everything is just magic, pulling coins from everywhere and cooking with lumps of grass . . . and I hate that stupid cat!'

'Is that a fact?' Hairy Angus dropped him in a heap. 'Well, Sheena,' he said with glittery, narrowed eyes. 'I think we should cast a wee spell on him, so he can't run away again.'

'No!' Jack yelled, terrified out of his mind. 'I promise, I won't do anything.'

'Give him another chance, Angus,' Sheena said. 'After all, he is my nephew.'

'Oh all right then,' Hairy Angus replied. 'But just one false move and he is history!'

'OK! OK!' Jack yelled.

Then he saw they were laughing.

'Have I just made a right idiot of myself?' he asked.

'You have,' they chortled.

'All this stuff is just another way of living. We like it better than the way folk live in the cities,' said Sheena. 'The grass is called peat, and the funny language is Gaelic, people often speak it up here.'

'That's why we sound different when we talk English, it's our nice wee accent,' Angus explained. 'You Glasgow folk sound just as silly to us.'

'And I use the broomstick to sweep up, not to fly on,' Sheena grinned. Jack could still see her teeth were pointy, but he didn't like to say anything.

'How about the coins and things?' he demanded.

'Conjuring tricks, Jack,' Hairy Angus said, pulling a fifty-pence piece from each ear.

'Oh.' Jack felt more and more stupid.

'You'll be fine, Jack, just relax and enjoy,' Sheena added kindly. 'OK?'

'OK,' he agreed sheepishly, then brightened, 'But only if Angus teaches me his tricks.'

'It's a deal,' Angus replied, whisking an apple from the air.

That night, the neighbours and their kids came round for a singsong. It wasn't too

bad, even if half the songs were in Gaelic and Jack couldn't understand a word. Sheena kept time by banging her broomstick on the floor while Hairy Angus played the fiddle.

Later, Jack knelt by the window of his room. The moon shone brightly on the sea. Suddenly he saw a great shadow fly across it. It looked just like Sheena with Pandor in front of her on the broomstick. 'Och no, Jack Baxter,' he said aloud. 'It's an owl. It has to be!' He blinked, but a cloud had drifted in. Only shadows were left.

'Hhmm, maybe I was right after all, whatever they say.' Jack slid down and covered his head with the covers. 'But if I'm going to survive this, I better not get too nosy!'

Weird singing started drifting in from the sea. He closed his eyes tight. OK, it might be the wind through the rocks, but you never can tell.

In the morning, Angus was waiting for him. 'Going fishing?' He tossed a pack of cards in the air and caught them in one hand. 'You can steer, then help me cast the line.'

'You're on!' Jack grabbed a couple of bits of bannock and ran down to where the boat tossed by the jetty. Above, the sun began to shine and the clouds faded like magic.

Later that day, he and some kids went swimming, then built fantastic barricades in the sand. Jack found some strings of smelly yellow seaweed and threw one at Euan, one of the boys from the cottage over the fields. He threw it right back.

'Let's have a seaweed fight!' somebody yelled and they began laughing and pelting one another till they all stank worse than Pandor's fish-head dinners. So they had another swim.

In the evening, he tried some soup and potato-cakes covered in butter. He wasn't sure if he liked them, so he ate six just to check. Angus conjured an apple cake out of Pandor's head for afters. Jack slept like a log that night without noticing a single eerie yowl.

Each day was an adventure, fishing, swimming, playing with the other kids and learning clever tricks from Angus until suddenly it was time to leave. Sheena handed him a bag full of the stuff she'd thrown into a box when he'd arrived. 'You might need this,' she said.

'Thanks.' He'd given up wondering about anything in this place.

Back in Glasgow he met up with his best mate, Graeme. 'So how did it go?' Graeme asked. 'Boring or what?'

'Och no,' Jack said with a secret grin. 'It wasn't a bit boring, as a matter of fact. My auntie's magic and so are her pals. Here, have you seen this wee trick?' He leaned over and took a ten-pence piece from Graeme's ear.

JOEY AND THE OTTER

Alan Temperley

Joey McKenzie was eight and he was fed up. He was fed up because his best friend, Alister, had gone away to live in Inverness. And he was fed up because his mum had just had a baby and no one had time for him any more.

The baby was a girl, which was bad enough, and there was something wrong with her. At least Joey thought there was, or did all babies cry like that and keep throwing up milk? The doctor came and the nurse. His mum fussed over her. And when his dad came home from the forestry, sawdust in his hair, all he had eyes for was baby Louise, toothless and wispy-haired, wrapped up in her bundle of white.

'Will you come out, Dad?' Joey spun his football.

'Maybe later, Joey.'

'Can we go fishing?'

His dad cradled Louise in the crook of his thick brown arm and held a bottle to her puckered lips. She twisted her head sideways. 'Not this week, son.'

Red-headed and freckled, Joey watched his dad try to press the bottle upon her.

Louise's tiny hands pushed him away. Her face scrunched up. She began to wail.

His mum joined them, tea towel in one hand. She looked anxious.

Joey went outside. Bran, their border collie, trotted at his heels. He was fed up too.

They lived in the Highlands, in a croft cottage between the hills and the sea. The village was two miles away. Joey's dad worked some sheep and went lobster fishing. It didn't bring in much money so he did seasonal work with the forestry. When Joey was at school his mum worked in the local hotel – at least she had until the arrival of Louise.

It was the May half-term and two days later Joey went fishing by himself. Rod in hand and bag bumping on his back, he climbed the heathery hillside and dropped down to the river beyond. It was a place he loved, the river pebbly and rocky, lined by a few crooked trees. A real wilderness with the hills rising above, not a house or a field in sight.

He tramped on upriver, wellies squelching in the marshy bits and splashing through the shallows. A heron flapped away. Early dragonflies skimmed about the rocks. He passed the muddy slide his dad had shown him where the otters skidded belly-down into the water.

Soon Joey reached the spot where he planned to begin fishing. Sitting on a lichen-covered boulder, he unearthed his tobacco tin of worms and threaded one on to his hook. Then, standing on a grassy hump that projected into the river, he cast to the far side of a peaty, beer-coloured pool.

Joey loved fishing and for an hour he was happy. His red and yellow float bobbed on the current. Steadily he worked downstream to the place where he had descended the hillside. Conditions were good, a little breeze and dappled cloud. He caught three trout, one so small he threw it back, but two half a pound or more. Holding the fish firmly, Joey cracked them over the back of the head with a stone. The trout leaped and shivered then were still.

He laid them on the heather to admire but his pleasure was mingled with sadness. They were bonny speckled fish. Just a minute earlier they had been darting in the cool shadows, quick and alive. He had dragged them out into the air, flapping and gaping. The only scar on their perfect bodies was the crushed skin where he had killed them. Still, he had come fishing and that's what fishing was. They would be good eating. His dad liked trout. His mum would be pleased. He dropped them into a supermarket bag, stowed it in his fishing bag and rebaited the hook.

Another half hour passed. Joey drank his juice and ate his biscuits. He began to feel lonely. Normally he went fishing with his dad or Alister. And though he had gone alone before, it was different when you had friends and fun to go back to. Now there was just his worried mum and the cries and nappies and curdled sick of Louise. At least if she'd been a boy she'd have grown up into someone for him to play with.

He trailed his bare feet in the water and wondered about going home. A short distance downstream the river narrowed between rocks and plunged away over a waterfall. At the bottom it ran through a ferny, tree-lined gorge for two hundred metres or so before emerging once more into the sunny glen. Joey had explored the gorge, though his mother had warned him not to, but never fished the deep black pool below the falls. He thought he'd give it a try.

As he picked his way downstream the roar of the waterfall grew louder. He stood on rocks at the brink and craned his neck to watch the speeding water vanish. The place where he would scramble down was fifty metres further on. Rod in one hand, he clutched a sapling with the other and skidded to a projecting boulder. The sides were steep but it was not *really* dangerous so long as he was careful. In a few minutes he was down, knees and bottom wet with earth, knuckle bleeding, but safe at the river's edge. It was colder down there, shadowy and green with twisted branches and thick moss. High above him the hillsides were bathed in sunshine but direct sunlight never penetrated to the bottom of the gorge. Joey liked it, it matched his mood.

He sucked his knuckle and clambered upstream to the pool below the waterfall. It was deep and scary. The drumming of the water echoed from wet, ferny cliffs on either side. Joey set down the fishing bag, baited his hook and cast across. At once the deep currents caught his line and pulled it this way and that, up towards the falling water, round, back again, and finally down to the shallows at the lower end. His worms washed ashore. Joey reeled in and cast again.

As he did so, his eye was attracted by something caught in the rocks not far from where his hook had ended up. It looked like a small animal. Drowned. What was it? Joey set his rod between two stones and scrambled closer to get a better look. Too big for a rat; too small for a dog. It rocked in the ripples, half caught on a bank of shingle and washed away on a swell of the current.

At that moment he saw what it was, a baby otter. And it moved, or he thought it did, though it wasn't swimming. The river carried it tail-first, then sideways, head under water. Joey tried to keep pace along the riverbank. Again he thought he detected movement, a twitch of the tail, the paddle of a leg. Briefly he hesitated then plunged into the river, way above his wellies, and forced his way across the current. The water rose to his hips. He nearly fell. The river swept the waterlogged bundle beyond his reach. He plunged after it. Momentarily it was trapped against a boulder. Joey reached out and just managed to grip one paw as it was carried away again.

Clutching the sodden creature against his jacket, he struggled ashore.

It was a pathetic little thing about half the size of a cat. Its fur hung in spikes, its eyes were closed, the broad muzzle was fringed with whiskers. He squeezed out some of the water and looked it in the face. A trace of warmth reached his fingers. The eyes cracked open. Joey was thrilled. But what should he do? The little animal had come over the waterfall, at least he assumed so. Was it badly hurt? He felt its legs and thick tail. Nothing seemed to be broken. But it was very weak.

And Joey was frozen. He scrubbed the cub as dry as he could and wrapped it in his jacket. Then he emptied his wellies, wrung out his jeans and pulled them back on. Carrying the cub beneath his jersey to warm it up, he returned to the pool to collect his rod.

Where was it? He looked all round. There lay his bag but his rod had gone. Then he saw it, three-quarters in the water, caught by the reel against a stone. Trying not to squash the cub, he picked it up and searched the pool for his float. It was nowhere to be seen. Abruptly a tremendous tug pulled the tip of his rod right down beneath the surface. The reel screamed. Joey got the fright of his life. Remembering what he had been taught, he lifted the rod high and reeled in as fast as he could. Again that terrific pull, then a huge fish leaped from the pool and fell back with a splash. Joey set his feet and reeled in again. Suddenly there was no resistance. The fish was gone. His float and a broken end of line skidded across the black water.

What a monster! Joey had never hooked such a fish. But he would have to come back another time for now he became aware of movement against his stomach. The baby otter was stirring. Carefully he lifted it out. The button-bright eyes were open. It made a half-hearted attempt to bite him and emitted a tiny cry.

Joey wondered what to do. If he left it in the cold gully where he had found it, it would likely die. If he took it home at least it would be warm and he could try it with some food. Maybe it would get strong again and he could make it into a pet. Otters made good pets. Something to make up for Alister and Louise. He settled it back under his jersey and tucked his jersey into his belt. Then, icy jeans tugging at every step, he clambered up from the gully.

It was two miles home. As he climbed the hillside his legs warmed up – and reaching the top he suddenly felt much warmer around his waist also. A faint smell reached his nostrils. Joey looked down. The otter had done both a pee and a pooh inside his jersey. Ugghh! He made a face but there was nothing to be done right then so he continued walking.

With so much news, he decided, he would

have to tell the truth: he had been down where his mum told him *never* to go. But when he reached home the house was empty. No sign of his mum or Louise. The car was gone. And his dad's work boots were in the lobby.

There was an arrangement: if his parents had to go out, Joey was to go to old Mrs Sutherland's down the road. But on this occasion, despite the cakes she gave him, Joey didn't want to go to Mrs Sutherland's. The house being empty suited him perfectly. He collected an old cardboard box from the garage, lined the bottom with newspaper and took the smelly cub from beneath his jersey.

It looked a bit better, its fur drying and turning fluffy, but still very weak. Again it gave that chirruping cry and tried to bite his fingers. Joey was too quick. Holding it across the back, he rinsed it in warm water in the sink, rubbed it dry on the kitchen towel and popped it into the box. One of his mum's cookery books held the top down.

It was time to clean himself. Trying to avoid touching his face, he peeled off his jersey and shirt and rinsed these too, then threw everything into the washing machine. He scrubbed his stomach clean with the dishcloth and flitted upstairs naked to put on dry clothes.

For the next hour Joey tried everything he could think of to get the cub to eat. He mixed formula milk in one of the baby's bottles and warmed it in the microwave as his mum did for Louise. The cub wouldn't touch it. Milk dripped from its muzzle. It became distressed. He tried cow's milk. He offered fish. And fish guts. He blended them with milk in the blender. He tempted it with milk in a dripper. He tried to feed it with a teaspoon and gave it food in a dish in the garage. It would eat nothing. He left it for a while and when he went back found it squeezing into a corner. He went to pick it up. A third time it tried to bite him and somehow ran past. By the time he caught it again the little creature was exhausted and in a panic, its heart racing beneath his fingertips.

Joey looked down at the neat ears and bristling whiskers and felt so sorry for it. He should never have brought it home, he realized that now. An otter would be a lovely pet but it wasn't fair. It was a wild thing, it didn't belong in a kitchen and garage, it belonged in the river with its mum. Probably it was still drinking her milk. Learning how to hunt. Perhaps if he took it back and left it by the otter slide one of the big otters would find it.

Joey threw out the gunge he had prepared so carefully and dumped the dishes in the sink. He didn't want to risk another pooh in his jersey so he lined the bottom of his fishing bag with a towel, forced the little creature inside and fastened the top so that it couldn't escape.

The wet socks and wellies had given him a blister. Limping in old trainers, he set off again across the hillside.

It seemed a long way but at last he reached the river. Joey walked on, twice sinking to his ankles in bogs. Soon he reached the otter slide. His bag moved and there was a sound of scratching. Joey opened it and wrinkled his nose at a familiar smell. Carefully he lifted out the baby otter and set it on a patch of shingle beside the river.

Would it swim? Would it wait? Joey did not know. For a while the cub hesitated, looking this way and that, and gave a little chirrup. Then tottering on weak legs, it hid among some rocks covered with tufty grass.

Joey could see it in the shadows. 'Bye-bye.' Reluctantly he turned away and pretended to leave. A rough knoll stood on the riverbank. Joey ducked behind it and crawled to the top from where he could watch what happened, if anything.

He lay on dead bracken. The cub's faint

peep reached him above the sounds of the river.

For a long time nothing significant occurred: a dipper flew from rock to rock, insects crawled before his nose, a pair of buzzards wheeled high overhead.

Time and again Joey nearly went home. He began to retreat. Then he heard a thin, high-pitched whistle. He scrambled back and stared, sharpening his eyes. A little line of bubbles crossed the river. He held his breath. Thirty metres away a full-grown otter emerged from the water. It stood in the shallows looking all round then advanced up the shingle.

The cub emerged from its hiding place and took a few uncertain steps. It froze. The adult otter sniffed it all over. Joey watched anxiously. Would the big otter accept it or reject it – even kill it? All seemed well. The baby relaxed and wandered away. The adult tumbled it over and snuffled into its fur. For a minute they played on the tiny beach then the big otter picked up the baby in its mouth and started back across the river.

A clump of twisted birch trees stood on the far bank. Beneath were water-washed roots and a tumble of giant boulders. The otter pulled itself from the river, set down the cub, shook itself on a rock, picked up the cub again and vanished into the shadows.

Joey waited a few minutes longer but no otter reappeared. The excitement was over. Bursting with news, he turned for home.

'The falls pool?' his dad said when Joey told him about the monster fish. 'Haven't been there for years.'

'Did you go down when I specifically told you not to?' said his mum but she wasn't angry.

'A baby otter?' his dad said. 'Good for you, Joey.'

'I wondered what all that was in the sink.' His mum's eyes were red with crying.

They weren't interested in his news. Baby Louise was in hospital. They had been with her all day. Something inside was twisted. She would have to have an operation.

They had left a note for him in the living room. When Joey brought the otter home he hadn't gone into the living room.

His excitement evaporated. The baby was sick. All at once everything he had done seemed unimportant. He looked at the scatter of baby photos on the sideboard. His tiny sister, blotched and goggle-eyed, swathed in white. Helpless. Suddenly he felt so sorry for her and put an arm round his mum's waist. She kissed the top of his head.

While she cleared up after dinner, his dad pulled Joey to his side on the settee. 'You've been having a rough time, son.' He put an arm round his shoulders. 'It's just wee Louise, you know.'

Joey took his dad's fingers. 'Will she be all right?'

'Yeah, course.' He smiled confidently.

Joey wasn't fooled.

'Don't worry yourself,' his dad said. 'Tell me about this otter. Where'd you say you found it exactly?'

So Joey told his dad his adventures.

'I'm right proud of you,' his dad said. 'You know that, Joey? Got a bit of spirit. What say when Louise is better we go down and have a crack at that fish?'

Joey smiled up as he knew his dad wanted.

At half past six they drove back to the hospital. Louise was in an oxygen tent. A clear plastic tube disappeared up one nostril. She was sound asleep.

For the first time Joey felt a surge of affection. She looked so weak and vulnerable.

'Can I put my hand in?'

The nurse smiled and nodded. Even though she was sound asleep, Louise's tiny hand closed on his forefinger. He moved it and she clung tight. He looked up at his mum.

'Don't worry, Mrs McKenzie,' the nurse said. 'It's just a wee operation. She'll be fine.'

And she was. A week later Louise was home.

And the Saturday after that, as Joey was holding his sister in an armchair giving her a bottle, his dad said: 'How about going after that fish when you've finished. And you can show me where the otters live.'

'OK.' Joey rocked the bottle. 'Keep your voice down, she's nearly asleep.'

SHOWTIME

Julie Bertagna

The street sparkled, as if scattered with diamonds. But it was only broken glass, glittering in the bright morning sun. The glass fragments crunched underfoot as Mo ran across the street. If only the street *were* full of diamonds. He'd stuff his pockets full of them. Then he'd be all right. Then everything would be all right.

Mo knew exactly what he would do if he had a pocketful of diamonds. He looked past the tall, grey tower blocks where he now lived, all across the city to the faraway purple smudges on the horizon. Those purpley shadows were hills and mountains, so like the ones in his own country. If he had money, that's where he would go – away out of the city, to live in the quiet of the hills and mountains. Maybe there, he and his family could live in peace at last.

'Hurry up, Mohammed!' shouted Moona, his older sister. 'We'll be in trouble if we're late.'

Mo hurried up a bit, but he didn't really care whether he was late or not. He was always in trouble. Every day was trouble.

He was never in trouble with the teachers.

His school jotters were sprinkled with gold and silver stars and smiley faces. *Very good*, Mrs Andrews would write. *Keep trying!* Mrs Andrews was kind. She seemed to know how hard things were for him. Mrs Andrews made sure he was safe in class but she couldn't keep him safe in the playground, or outside school.

'Come *on*!' yelled Moona, as the bell rang.

Mo kicked an empty cola can and heard it clang on the school railings as he ran through the gate. He thought of the long day ahead and felt sick.

The morning started off much better than Mo expected. Mrs Andrews put him and Sarah at a small table on their own where they worked together, learning spellings from their word tins. Sarah was nice. She was never horrible to him. But she could only do baby work, just like Mo. The other children were in groups named after wild animals like the Tigers or the Bears. Sarah and Mo were supposed to be in the Lions, but really, Mo thought, they were the Stupid Sheep.

He had never been stupid before. At school in his own country, he had always been one of the cleverest in his class. It was just that everything here was so different.

The whole language was different. Mo was learning English as fast as he could, but it wasn't fast enough to keep up with the other children. He wasn't stupid, but everyone thought he was.

But he would show them. He would learn their language as fast as he could. Then they might stop picking on him.

Now, just as he was calm and happy and settled in his work, just as he was thinking he might have quite a good day after all, an ear-splitting noise erupted that frightened Mo so much it jolted him out of his seat.

It was the rising wail of a siren. Mo dived for cover under his school desk, as he had been taught to do at that sound. With his heart hammering hard in his chest, he heard the other children laughing. From his hiding place under the desk Mo could see the other children's feet line up at the classroom door. Why were they laughing? Didn't they understand the danger? Hadn't they been taught to hide from attack?

Mrs Andrews's navy-blue shoes appeared at the desk beside him. Then his teacher's concerned face was suddenly under the desk, beside his own terrified one.

'It's all right, Mohammed. It's just a fire drill. There's no danger. We're all safe.'

The teacher took his hand and gently

pulled him out from under the desk. All around him, the other children were giggling and laughing. Mrs Andrews told them to be quiet as they filed out of the classroom and into the playground. They quietened down but they didn't stop.

Mad Mohammed, they whispered and sniggered. *Mad Mo, the asylum seeker.*

'Mad Mo should be in an asylum,' said William, kicking him on the ankle, as soon as Mrs Andrews wasn't looking. 'That's where they put mad people, in madhouses and asylums. My dad says all you asylum seekers should go back to your own country or be put away in asylums.'

Mad Mo, the asylum seeker. That's what they called him. That's why they hated him and wouldn't leave him in peace.

He and his family had fled their own country to escape a war, only to find they were at war with the people of this new land. At least that's what it felt like. Mo had never understood what the war in his own country was about. His mother said she didn't understand either why people had to fight and hate each other, why they couldn't learn to live together. Mo and his family thought they had left the war behind them. All they had done was swap the enemy at home for this new one in a strange land.

All the way home, Mo searched for beer and fizzy drink cans to use instead of a football. He kicked them fiercely, making each one clang noisily against walls and railings, imagining he was scoring goal after goal against a rival team.

'Stop doing that!' warned Moona, as they passed a crowd of teenagers at the shop. 'You're asking for trouble.'

'I get trouble whether I ask for it or not,' Mo shouted at her. He could say whatever he liked to Moona, in their own language. No one else understood. But Moona looked worried as the teenagers turned to stare at them, so Mo stopped firing goals all around and contented himself with dribbling an empty beer can noisily up the street.

'Not bad, kid,' one of the boys shouted over.

Mo looked over warily. His wariness turned to astonishment as the older boy grinned at him.

'We could do with you playing for Scotland,' the boy added.

'He's one of those asylum seekers they've put in the high flats,' said one of the other boys.

'I don't care if he's a Martian from outer space. He plays football better than most of the Scotland team. They're useless. Keep it up, kid!'

The boy gave him another grin and Mo found himself grinning back. He was still grinning when he got into the lifts beside Moona.

'What are you looking so pleased with yourself for?' she smiled, pleased to see him happy for once, as she pressed the button for the twenty-second floor.

'Did you hear what that boy said? I'm sure he said I was good enough to play for Scotland,' Mo told her.

'Well, *he* must be mad if he thinks that,' Moona laughed.

*

It was silly, he knew, but what the boy said stuck in Mo's mind. Imagine if one day he really could play for Scotland, he kept telling himself. It didn't matter to Mo that this wasn't his own country. He would play for anyone, even a team of Martians from outer space – just as long as he could play football.

Next to the home and family and friends he had left behind when he and Moona and their parents had fled the war, football was the thing he missed most. He used to spend hours every day after school out in the dusty streets, kicking anything that could be kicked – stones, tin cans, bits of litter; anything at all that could be used as a football. Mo used to have a real football, but when the soldiers arrived in the village they had taken whatever they wanted – and his football had been one of the things they had taken, and never given back.

Here, a can had a quite different sound when kicked. It gave a hard clatter and clank as it hit the tarmac streets and pavements. In his homeland, a tin-can football made gentler dings and clangs as he kicked it through the dusty streets and fields. He missed home so much. He missed the wide valley and the mountains all around it, the bright-painted houses and the huge plane trees in the village square where the old people brought their kitchen chairs out and sat and talked and watched the world, shaded from the sun, from early morning till late at night.

In summer, even when darkness fell, the old people sat out under the trees. Mo would lie in bed listening to them and fall asleep to the sound of their voices. It made him feel safe.

But there came a time when the soft night-time chatter was replaced by the *crak-crak* of gunfire that echoed from mountain to mountain and all around the valley. The old people, along with the rest of the villagers, huddled under beds and in cellars. No one could sleep. No one felt safe.

Mo got up from the sofa where he and his family were sitting watching TV. He went over to the window and looked down to the ground, far below. Here, it was often rainy, too wet to play outside, but even when it wasn't his parents still wouldn't let him go out. They were too scared that he would come to harm.

Far down below his window in the tower block was the green rectangle of the school football pitch. Mo could just make out the tiny figures of the school football team upon it. William and his gang were all in the football team so it was no use. They would never let him near the pitch, never mind play. He would never be able to persuade them. Mo looked longingly down at the pitch. What could he do?

Next day at school, as soon as he and Sarah were set to work on their word tins, Mo leaned over. He felt close to bursting. He had to talk to someone and Sarah was the only one there was.

'Football,' he said.

Sarah looked up at him in surprise. She

had tried to speak to Mo lots of times, but although he was beginning to understand more English, they couldn't talk about very much because he spoke so little of his new language. But sometimes they talked in pictures. Sarah would draw a picture of a clockface showing half past three, the end of the school day, and Mo would draw a crazily smiling face beside it, which made them both smile.

Now Mo drew a picture of a football then a love heart beside it. Then he pointed to himself.

'You love football?' guessed Sarah.

'Yes,' said Mo. Then he drew a green rectangle with a tiny football on it and lots of tiny stick figures running about on it.

Sarah wrinkled up her face, puzzled.

'I want football,' said Mo.

'Oh,' said Sarah. 'You want to *play* football.'

'I want to *play* football!' echoed Mo. He drew a question mark.

'You don't know how to play football?' asked Sarah.

Mo sighed. He drew another stick figure with a football at his feet and wrote his own name above it. Next, he drew a great big star beside the stick boy. Finally, he wrote *VERY GOOD* in huge letters inside the star.

Sarah smiled. 'You are very good at football,' she read. 'You love it. You want to play it. Well, why can't you play it? What's stopping you?'

Mo looked over to the table where William and his bullying gang sat.

Sarah nodded. She understood. In a picture story, Sarah had told him that before he had come to the school, it was Sarah who had borne the brunt of William's bullying.

'Please help,' Mo said quietly.

Sarah's face flushed and she looked pleased. Mo knew why. Nobody ever asked Sarah for help. No one ever thought she *could* help. She was always the one who had to ask Mrs Andrews or one of the other children for help with anything from tying her shoelaces to remembering what day of the week it was. Mo doubted if Sarah could help him but she was the only person he could ask – apart from Mrs Andrews. But, kind though she was, the teacher was always so busy. If he tried to explain to Mrs Andrews what he wanted he would have to try to hurry up and then he would panic and forget the words or muddle them all.

Now, Sarah was wrinkling her face again, just as she did over her word tin every day when she was concentrating hard. She chewed her lip. Then all of a sudden her arm shot up into the air. She waggled it about excitedly and let out little gasping squeaks to get the teacher's attention.

'Yes, Sarah?' said Mrs Andrews. 'What's the problem?'

'*Please* can we do "Showtime" after our work, Mrs Andrews? Please!'

Mrs Andrews smiled in surprise. Sarah hardly ever spoke out in school. She never brought things to show the rest of the class. She was too shy. 'Have you something interesting to show us, Sarah?'

'No, Mrs Andrews,' said Sarah, 'but Mo has.'

Mrs Andrews turned to Mo in even greater surprise. 'Have you, Mo?'

Mo looked at Sarah blankly then at Mrs Andrews. He shook his head.

'Yes, he has, he has!' insisted Sarah. 'But we need to go out on to the football pitch to see what it is.'

Mrs Andrews looked from Sarah to Mo in bewilderment. A slow, wide grin was spreading all over his face.

'On to the football pitch?' she said doubtfully.

'Yes!' said Mo and Sarah together.

Mo could hear William and the others who picked on him, who had made his life a misery from the first day he had arrived at the school, muttering that he was Mad Mo, he should be locked up in an asylum. But the rest of the children were smiling at him, delighted to be going outside instead of being stuck in the classroom till breaktime.

Mrs Andrews laughed. 'Well, all right. Finish up your work, everyone, then we'll go and see what Mo has to show us.'

Sarah had brought a ball from the gym hall. She handed it to Mo.

'You just *show* them, Mo,' she said, and made a face in the direction of William and his gang, who were yawning loudly and acting as if this was the most boring event in the world.

Mo got ready. All of a sudden he felt stupid. What was he doing? He would never get into the school football team. It didn't matter how good he was. They would rather let a Martian from outer space play for the team than Mad Mo, the asylum seeker. He sighed. Then he heard the plane.

Whenever a plane flew overhead, Mo took fright in the same way he had when the school fire alarm went off. In his home village, planes had been things to run from – to run from for your life. Now, as the noise of the plane grew, Mo felt his heart fill with that familiar old terror and he wanted to run and hide. He turned and saw the shadow of the plane's huge wings touch the edge of the school playground, moving fast towards the football pitch where he stood. Mo turned, threw the ball down and began to run.

As soon as the football hit the ground, Mo knew where he was running. He was running for the ball. It was the only thing he could do. As the shadow of the plane came towards him he scooped up the ball with his foot and began dribbling it fast and hard, as if an enemy was on his tail. Expertly, he dodged around imaginary opponents, one after another, all over the pitch. When the shadow was almost upon him, he was far away from the goal, deep in the centre of the field, but he had to try.

Mo lined up the ball with his foot and his eyes. He aimed, whacking the ball with all the strength he had. Then he closed his eyes.

The sound of cheering made him open then. Sarah was dancing along the sidelines of the pitch, jumping up and down, clapping her hands in the air like a cheerleader. Mrs Andrews was beaming at him in astonishment. William and his gang stood looking awkward and stupid. The rest of the class had begun to chant his name. Mo's heart sank. It didn't matter what he did he would always be Mad Mo, the asylum seeker. Then he heard the words.

Mo! Mo! Super-Mo!

With a huge grin, Mo ran to collect the football from the net. For the first time since he had arrived in Scotland, he felt right at home.

Interesting things you probably didn't know about the authors . . .

Ann McDonagh Bengtsson

Ann McDonagh Bengtsson was born in a mining village in the west of Scotland. With her parents, who were teachers, long school holidays were spent year after year exploring the Highlands and Islands, come wind, rain or glorious shine. The legendary Isle of Skye was a particular favourite where she got to know a lot of fun people and where, in her story, 'Jack's Auntie's Magic!', Jack finds out that there's more magic to life than he ever guessed back home in Glasgow!

Julie Bertagna

Julie Bertagna was born in Ayrshire and grew up near Glasgow. She has worked as a magazine editor, a teacher and a freelance journalist. She writes for children and for young adults and one of her books, *The Ice-Cream Machine*, is being developed for television. Julie lives in Glasgow with her family, close to lots of music stores, second-hand bookshops and coffee bars.

Visit her web site on www.juliebertagna.com

Theresa Breslin

Theresa Breslin has written lots of books for young people, including the popular and funny *Dream Master* series. She loves sharing stories and discussing books with anyone who will listen. *Simon's Challenge* was filmed for television and *Whispers in the Graveyard* won the Carnegie Medal. Check out her web site (www.theresabreslin.com) for more information and fun activities on reading and writing.

Lindsey Fraser

I was born and brought up in Scotland, and some of my happiest and funniest memories are of family holidays in the Highlands and Islands.

'Each to Their Own' isn't a true story, but it owes a great deal to my memories, the people involved and hours spent collecting shells.

I have always worked in the field of children's literature – with teachers, librarians, parents and children – and I enjoy finding different ways to bring books and young people together. Recently I have written two author biographies and edited two anthologies of short stories, including *Stories from Scotland* (Macmillan Children's Books).

Vivian French

Vivian French was best known at school for talking too much. She continued her attachment to words by becoming first an actor, then a storyteller and finally a writer of children's books . . . she's not sure how many she's written, but more than a hundred. She now travels all over the world, telling stories and swapping ideas about books and writing with children and adults. PS She still talks too much.

Keith Gray

Keith's first book, *Creepers*, was published when he was twenty-four, and it went on to be shortlisted for the Guardian Fiction Prize. Since then he has written several novels for children and young adults including *Happy*, *The Runner* and *Warehouse*. He lives in Edinburgh with a cockatiel called Baxter.

Jackie Kay

Jackie Kay was born in Edinburgh and brought up in Glasgow. She writes for children and for adults, fiction and poetry. She has a son called Matthew. She lives in

Manchester. Her first novel for children *Strawgirl* is published by Macmillan this year.

Joan Lingard

Joan Lingard was born in Edinburgh but grew up in Belfast, where she lived from age two to eighteen. She is the author of fourteen novels for adults and more than forty books for children. She has received a number of awards, both in Germany and the UK, including, in 1998, the MBE for Services to Children's Literature.

Website: www.joanlingard.co.uk.

Catherine MacPhail

I was lying in bed one Sunday and I opened up the paper and there was yet another worthy article about saving the planet. I closed it quickly and suddenly, in my head, I heard a teacher asking in a shocked voice, 'Aren't you interested in saving the planet?' A cheeky wee voice answered her, 'But Amazonian rainforests, Miss. That's got to be the most boring subject in the world.' Right away I knew I had two characters I wanted to write about – a teacher with a secret and a wee boy who really does save the planet. I love it when stories come to you like that. Hope it never stops.

Janet Paisley

I write poems, plays, stories, films and for radio and television. I write almost all the time, especially when I'm not sleeping. When I sleep, I dream and that's a kind of writing too. I write for grown-ups as well. But I like writing for children because I was one, once, and I liked stories and poems. When I grew up, I made my own children. Six of them. All boys. I liked telling and reading them stories and poems. Now they're grown-up so I write for other people's children. You, in fact.

I wrote 'Porridge and Me' because I didn't like porridge when I was small but my mum said it was good for me. I hope this porridge is good for you.

Alison Prince

Alison Prince has written over forty children's books. She lives on the Isle of Arran, which she says is the sanest mad place in the world. She has three grandchildren and two cats, and plays the clarinet in a jazz band.

Frank Rodgers

'Write a story about Scottishness,' said Polly the editor.

'Scottishness?' I asked. 'What's that, by the way?'

'You tell me,' she replied.

So I sat down and chewed it over (along with my Scotch pie and chips and a couple of deep-fried Mars bars). I came to the conclusion that Scottishness – or Englishness, Swissness or Danishness for that matter – is a bit like a big Pick 'n' Mix . . . a combination of different *flavours*. Dipping my hand into the bag marked 'West of Scotland', I came up with these things . . . the weather, football, fast food, tribalism and optimism . . . all dusted with a touch of magic.

Margaret Ryan

Margaret Ryan used to be a teacher but gave it up because she didn't like sums. She lives in an old mill with her husband John, a collection of teddy bears and a multi-coloured dinosaur called Spike. She has two very sensible, grown-up children. When Margaret grows up, she's going to be sensible too. Probably.

Alan Temperley

Alan was born and grew up in Sunderland. As a boy he kept mice, sang in a big church choir, played cricket and rugby, enjoyed stories and knocked around on his bike. As a grown-up he had been a merchant seaman, a teacher of English and an author. His two wishes are that you will live life to the full and that you will be kind to all animals.

If you enjoyed this yummy selection of Scottish stories, you'll also like:

Stories from Scotland

Edited by Lindsey Fraser and Kathryn Ross

From Scotland past and present come runaway bannocks, know-it-all dads, cake-guzzling fairies, bothersome bikes and a fur coat filled with fivers.

All these and more can be found in this cracking anthology of Scottish stories, ideal for reading aloud, reading alone or reading with family and friends.

*If you enjoyed this yummy selection of Scottish stories,
why not try some scrumptious Scottish poems?*

Scottish Poems

Chosen by John Rice

A whistle-stop tour of Scottish poetry, offering a
brilliant mix of the modern, the old, the familiar and
the unknown.

A special treat for everyone!

If you enjoyed this yummy selection of Scottish stories, why not try some Irish ones as well?

GIANTS OF THE SUN
An anthology of Irish writing

Edited by Polly Nolan

A brilliant book bursting with spooky shipwrecks and smiling giants, dark tunnels and burning houses, tricked teachers and sparkly seasides, strange aliens and odd things in puddles.

An explosion of super stories from Ireland's very best writers.